Misshapen Angels

Case 1: Nekomata

Author: Joshua Koehn
Editor: Ashley Owca
Cover Art: Hydroxide Art (hydroxideart.carrd.co)

Dedicated to every kid still trying to find their place in the world.

Chapter 1

Rain lightly spattered on the windshield of the green sedan as it drove down the empty highway. The driver, dressed in a plain t-shirt and jeans, took his eyes off the road for a second and peered through his glasses at the cell phone mounted to the dashboard. The bright display, which was currently directing him, showed the turn off he needed was just ahead and his destination was a few blocks from that. He had not seen a building for miles, but the information the phone had produced, assured him where he was going was still there. He looked down at the arrival time to make sure it hadn't changed, and the driver hoped he had timed everything properly. He was past the point of no return and had to fight through the anxiety that had begun to build up.

"Could you please keep your eyes on the road, Jon?" The tall, thin, and bald man, who was dressed in a black suit and sat in the passenger seat, requested flatly. "I would prefer not to die tonight if at all possible."

"Well, Caine," Jon started as he made the turnoff, "if you would help and navigate for me, I wouldn't need to check the damn thing. Instead, you're probably over there asleep."

"I'm just going over what intel I have on this place." The man's long, thin fingers continued to tap against his cell phone's screen, just as they had since he got in the car. Jon could only catch glimpses of the screen's reflections in Caine's sunglasses. It was just a pure white screen, but Caine continued to navigate it without a hint of trouble.

"Anything good?" Jon asked, rolling down the window to allow the night air in. He pulled a cigarette out of a pack stuffed in the console to his side and lit it using the old car's built-in lighter.

"Nothing seems out of the ordinary," The man closed what was on his phone and tucked the object into the inner breast pocket of his suit. "I have a list of employees, wages and tips, along with their regular dancers. Nothing strange aside from a new dancer, but any place worth its weight would have a rotating cast, so to speak. Bills herself as Mistress Valentine. Says she has horns."

"I've overheard one of my students talk about this place." Jon shrugged as he puffed the smoke out the window. "What they've said seemed too specific to be bullshit. Maybe we go in and find what we are looking for. If it ain't there, we don't and just enjoy a beer and a show."

"You just wanted a drinking partner for the night." Caine's pale face and almost invisible lips broke into a slight smile.

"If I wanted that I would have just hung out at Misshapen all night." Jon shook his head as he began to look for signs of his destination. "Run up my tab there."

Jon pulled the car into a dirt patch. Based on the number of other cars there it had to be the parking lot of the

2

gentlemen's club before them. As he pulled into a spot, he noticed that for being in the middle of nowhere, the place was quite busy. The two men sat for a moment in the car. Neither moving. Jon continued to work on his cigarette, while Caine said nothing. He just stared forward with an statuesque, blank stare.

"Planning on sending in a scout?" Caine spoke, finally breaking the silence.

"No," Jon declined the idea. He then peered left, right and behind him. He counted the cars in his head. "We're outnumbered anyway. We are just going to see if what I heard was true, then leave. We'll come back later if we need to."

The two men stepped out of the car. Caine towered over Jon as the two walked to the trunk of the vehicle. Jon had guessed that the man, who was built like a basketball player, had to be pushing seven feet which, was about a foot taller than himself. He often wondered where he got suits tailored to fit him. After knowing the man for as many years as he did, he always found that it was better not to ask questions about anything relating to his comrade. If Caine wanted to say something, he would.

Jon rummaged around the back until he found an old, beat up lockbox. He smacked the side of the box with the palm of his hand. The lid sprung open and revealed a wad of cash stowed away inside. Without counting it, Jon silently handed it to the tall man and closed the trunk.

Caine stuffed the money in a side pocket of his coat and began to head to the door. He stopped when he noticed he was not being followed. Jon stayed by the car, leaning up against it, finishing his cigarette. Slowly, he would inhale the smoke, and then let it out of his lungs even slower. Caine returned to the car and stood by his much smaller companion.

"Nervous?" Caine's cold and calm voice sounded flat even when he tried to crack a joke.

"No." Jon tossed the tobacco on the ground and rubbed the smoldering embers with his foot to make sure it was out. He ran his fingers through his medium length black hair and sighed. "Taxes keep going up on those things. I don't want to waste any of it."

"Understandable." Caine nodded and the two of them headed towards the front door of the place.

A bored, fat man in a black shirt, with the club's name cheaply printed on the front, set down his book as the two approached.

"Need to see some ID." The bouncer greeted the two. Jon pulled out his wallet and quickly obliged. The fat man shined a flashlight on it, and then quickly into Jon's face confirming the license he was handed was in fact of the man in front of him. He nodded and handed it back to Jon. Caine stood still and unmoving. He then reached in his pocket and pulled out 50 dollars and handed it to the man. The bouncer shinned the light on the money, then in the face of the man dressed in black. He pocketed the money and nodded the two inside.

"Have a good night," Jon wish the bouncer as the two went in.

"I'm surprised your fake ID continues to work," Caine said as the two were alone in a neon red hallway. "Cash tends to open more doors and create fewer questions."

"Your being a giant seems to help a lot too," Jon stated as the two entered the main floor. "People tend to question you more when they think they can kick your head in."

Jon found a table near a door to what he guessed was a kitchen. The same red neon hue adorned the entire place. An elevated, black dance floor sat in the middle and people

4

were all gathered around, ready to throw money at who was about to come up next. Caine took his leave to the bar and left Jon alone in the shadows, further away from the dance floor.

"Ladies and Gentlemen, please give a rousing greeting to our newest dancer. She is ready to keep you all in line. Bow down before Mistress Valentine!"

Jon leaned back in his seat. He smiled to himself. Right on time.

A sleazy sounding heavy metal song blared to life to introduce a blonde woman with a riding crop, who split the curtain to the stage. She was tall, leggy, and her attitude dominated the entire room, as she marched on stage in beat to the song. Fishnets and vinyl "fuck me" boots covered two tattooed legs. The black vinyl mini skirt was just like what many of Jon's professors in college had described in essays; long enough to cover everything, but short enough to keep it interesting. The leather biker jacket seemed slightly too big for her, but that probably wouldn't matter soon. Her eyes were golden and to say the least, enchanting. What was most unusual about the woman, however, was her forehead. Two horns were protruding from it and both looked rough and mangled. The one on the left side of her head was thin and looked like it was ready to be easily snapped at any time. The one on the right was much sturdier but was bent and looked like if it grew too much bigger, it would begin to drive into the side of her skull.

Jon watched with great interest as she moved and danced. One man at the end of the stage quickly threw money onto the platform. The woman marched over and didn't pick it up. She looked down at the man and sat down atop the cash. She stared deep into him and stuck her legs out on the bar which separated the dancer's stage from the customers. The man quickly tried to stuff more in her boot but a quick swat to the hand with the riding crop stopped him. She put one leg on each of the man's shoulders and told him to "lick them before putting his dirty money in there." The man gladly obliged and took his time doing it. After he tipped her again, the woman leaned back and put her hands behind her on the stage. Then, using the bar as leverage, she slowly flipped herself into a handstand, placed her feet underneath her one at a time until she was upright, and turned back to the center of the stage.

"See something you like, mister?" A greasy man in a suit standing next to Caine interrupted the show for Jon. "Your friend tells me you'd like something a little more intimate than a lap dance. However, this being her first night, it will be a while before Mistress Valentine is on the menu."

"Too bad," Jon looked disappointed. "Because I have some very special tastes, and she looks like she is very unique."

"If unique is what you want," The man smiled big. "I might have something right up your alley."

Jon stood up. He took one more look at the dancer, who seemed to look his way and lick her black-painted lips. Jon returned a shy smile and followed the two suited men into the back.

As soon as Jon saw the back of the club, he felt that many of his suspicions were about to be confirmed. The stench of narcotics and body odor filled his nostrils. Various strong-looking men lined the hallways, not one of them even bothering to acknowledge the trio as they walked by. The walls were a mixture of drywall and bad plywood patch jobs. A carpet was laid down, but it already bore the stains of spilled drinks, dirt, and possibly bodily fluids Jon did not want to be identified.

The group passed a room with a dirty mattress on the floor and a camera posted in the corner. The next door they

6

passed, Jon could clearly hear a man grunting away and a woman very obviously faking an orgasm. Jon looked to his partner and without seeing his eyes, could tell that behind the sunglasses Caine was already scoping out the place. He was also taking note of the guards looking after it.

The three stopped by a door. Their escort pulled out a set of keys. After a bit of fumbling, he found the one that removed the padlock on the door. He then twisted the handle and pushed the door open to reveal a barely lit room.

"Go ahead and have a seat." The man gave a smile so slimy it was almost dripping. "You're companion for this evening will be right with you."

Jon walked into the room. Caine attempted to follow by was stopped by the escort. A guard near the door pulled a gun and while keeping it aimed at the floor. He then made room for himself between Caine and the door. Caine didn't show any signs of intimidation.

"You only paid for your friend and not for yourself, big guy." The escort patted Caine on the chest and left the guard to stand in between the tall man and the door. The guard folded his arms, but kept his finger off the trigger, and stared up at Caine. The man in the black suit did nothing but stare down at the guard. The escort locked the door and walked off, leaving the two staring holes into each other.

The room was much fancier than the one Jon had passed by earlier. A vanity sat against the wall with a large mirror flanked by two jars filled with bamboo. A comfortably soft looking bed was posted opposite them and was overflowing with too many pillows, but what looked like only one blanket. A handcuff lay cuffed to one of the bedposts where the finish had been rubbed off the wood by the metal. Something about how luxurious the room was made Jon extremely uncomfortable.

Going on his gut feeling he approached the mirror. He checked his teeth for any irregularities. As he finished, he straightened himself and backed away from the mirror. However, he forgot about the stool and placed his hand against the mirror to steady himself as he tripped. The edges were solidly against the wall, but the middle of the mirror bent in slightly with the pressure from his palm. The space behind it had to be hollow.

"Are you alright, my master?" A shy, soft voice came from behind Jon.

Jon quickly turned. A woman with black hair stood at the doorway. A long, red, silk-looking, kimono covered her body. The woman clung tightly to the sleeves and fiddled nervously with them. Jon could not tell much about her but noticed two striking features right away. Her eyes were a mixture of green and gold, with long vertical pupils, and poking up from atop her head were two grey cat ears, folded back.

"I'm fine," Jon let the woman know of his condition.

"I am told I am to take care of you this evening." The woman stated slowly. Her voice cracked slightly. She averted her eyes from Jon as he approached her. A wide, excitedly facinated smile crossed his face. The woman grew more and more uneasy and recoiled slightly as Jon reached out for her. He stopped himself upon noticing this.

"I thought you only existed in folklore," Jon whispered to himself more than the woman. His eyes began to wander as curiosity got the better of him. "Too bad I'm not allowed to touch."

"In this room," The woman gulped. "I am to take care of you however you wish. Even if that includes touching."

Jon lost his smile and moved his hand to the side of the woman's face. Her ears nervously flicked as his hand softly touched her face. He gently slid it up to where a human ear should be and found nothing. He couldn't help himself and let an amused grin play on the side of his lips. He felt her shudder as he touched her, and he lost his smile instantly.

"Then let me take your robe," Jon instructed the woman. She nodded submissively.

The woman froze up as Jon took the kimono off her and walked over to the vanity. He spread it out over the mirror and hung it up, blocking the entire thing.

"Don't want that to get wrinkled, do we?" Jon turned back to the woman. He noted how she only stood there in thin, torn lingerie. Goosebumps had begun to grow on her body. The bumps only made the various bruises stand out even more than they had against her pallor skin. Jon quickly snatched the blanket from the bed and wrapped it around her. He hoped this would give her more warmth compared to the robe.

"Does my body not please you?" The woman asked quietly.

"No," Jon spoke softly, quietly, and flatly. "There are too many bruises. That's why I'm getting you out of here."

The woman's breath stopped, and her eyes grew wide.

Chapter 2

Mistress Valentine had finished her dance, collected her cash, and made her way to the back. The other dancer coming on next subtly tried to trip her as the two passed. From behind the curtain, Valentine threw up a middle finger behind her back at the woman without breaking her own stride. She knew the other dancer could not see it, but it made herself feel better.

In the dressing area, she tossed the pile of discarded clothes in a locker where her other personal items were and took a seat. She began to count out the wad of cash she had received and then quickly stuffed it in the boot that was licked "clean" earlier.

She stood back up when a small vibration caught her attention from her locker. She pulled a cell phone off the shelf. It was a simple text message. She sighed, responded, set it back down and started to throw the clothes she had taken off earlier, back on. She had not brought anything except for one outfit but figured she could supplement it with something from the wardrobe they kept on site.

Valentine looked around to find it and noted she was the only person in the room. She pushed a few articles of clothing on the rack down and out of her way. She couldn't help but feel disappointed when she found nothing to fit her tastes. That was until she looked in the locker of the woman who tried to trip her. A leather biker hat, adorned with a silver chain, sat on a shelf. She tried it on and looked at herself in the mirror. The hat no longer belonged to that bitch; it was now hers.

Before she could sit back down and relax, the door to the dressing room opened and the man who escorted the tall guy and his friend to the back walked in. Mistress Valentine fought the urge to gag at the smell of his sweat and incredibly cheap cologne.

"Enjoying your first night here?" The man grinned, taking the view of the woman in as she continued to dress in the vinyl and leather, she had just taken off moments ago. He secretly wished she would slow down as she pulled her skirt up.

"Made some decent money," the woman responded, uninterested in what the guy had to say.

"I can tell you a quick way to make even more." The man took a seat in the chair where she had been sitting earlier to count her cash.

"I'm listening." Valentine cocked an eyebrow.

"There's something special about you," The man pointed a greasy finger at her. "The eyes, the horns. Those ain't props and contacts. Props would look better than those."

"Fuck you," The woman spat.

"Sorry," The man held his hands up. "Didn't mean to offend. I was just making a point."

"Then get to it." The woman's disdain for the man grew the longer he was in her presence.

"I serve a very select clientele here," The man leaned back in his chair. "Some with some very particular tastes. Tastes for things like you. So, you give a private dance, shoot a video, whatever it takes. You make a shit ton of cash. Not only that, but I got whatever you need to keep you in a party mood."

"Drugs and money?" Valentine asked to confirm what he was talking about.

"Weed, smack, and coke are in high supply," The man pulled a small baggie of white powder out of his breast pocket and opened it. He made two short lines on the table with it. Using a metal tube he had produced from his pocket, he snorted one deep and sighed heavily. He then tried to hand the tube to the dancer. "Shit's clean as snow on the Rockies. Want some?"

"I'm much more interested in the cash," the woman coldly declined the material goods..

"Well, then," The man stood up, did the second line, and wiped his nose with his thumb. "Let's go talk in my private office."

The two walked down a barely lit hallway. Mistress Valentine tried to keep her hands to herself. The place was dirty enough she was afraid of catching something. They made their way past a few guards including one that appeared to be having a staring contest with a tall man in a black suit.

The businessman, already starting to get jitters from the coke, opened a door at the end of the hall. A red leather couch sat on one side of the room, with a desk in the center. The walls were draped with what looked like cheap curtains. The desk was bare aside from two candles on either end of the desk, and a box of cigars.

"Why don't you have a seat on the couch." The man gestured to Valentine. She pushed past him and took a seat on his desk.

"This is my audition, right?" The woman motioned for him to have a seat in his office chair. "Then come over here and see what I can do."

The man felt powerless as he did exactly what he was told. The Mistress crossed her legs as the man got close and stared down at him. Using the tip of her boot, she separated the man's legs and placed her foot between them on the chair. Not breaking eye contact, she reached over and opened the box of cigars. She placed one in her mouth, bit the tip off and spat it at the man.

She smiled as she watched him. The man was engrossed by her, and even that was an understatement. A small bit of drool came out the corner of his mouth. Valentine lit the cigar with a lighter from the box, took a drag to make sure it would stay lit and used it to wipe up the man's saliva as she placed the cigar in the man's mouth. She then lit the two candles next to her.

Slowly and gently, she took the man's hand and used it to unzip her leather jacket and reveal her lithe, tight body; she was covered only by a skin-tight leather bra underneath. She took off the hat she wore and placed it on her viewer's head. She leaned back and ran her fingers softly down her stomach as, leading his eyes right to where she wanted them to be. The man tried to reach out, but Mistress Valentine swatted his hand away. She moved the point of her boot a little deeper into the man's crotch and gave him a stern look.

Valentine continued the pressure as she continued the performance. She took one of the candles and licked her lips as she began to drip wax in her navel. She jumped slightly, revealing her abdominal muscles as it hit her alabaster skin.

14

"You see, sir," The woman cooed as she let a few more drops land over the tops of her breasts. "I would never join your little harem. Money would be nice, but I'm just not that kind of girl."

The man said nothing as Valentine climbed down off the table and straddled him. She reached in her mouth and pulled on her teeth. Two sets of dentures came out in her hand that revealed two rows of jagged, carnivorous teeth underneath.

"Because unfortunately for you, I have a nice, long, life span," The woman placed her hand over the man's mouth, snapped her head down and bit into the side of his neck. She almost squealed in ecstasy as hot blood began to fill her mouth. She then threw her head back and tore a chunk of flesh out, spilling blood down the front of his shirt. More blood dripped from out of her mouth and down the front of her body. She spit the flesh out in her hand and held it in front of the man in the now bloody suit. "And I think your lifespan is just too short."

Valentine climbed off and kicked the man's chair over as he twitched. The gasping screams began to come as he tried to force himself away from his assailant. The woman stood there, dangled the flesh in front of herself, and like a bird with multiple quick snaps, swallowed the flesh she had taken.

She paid the man no mind as he struggled on the floor and eventually passed out. Valentine took the candles and put them to the cheap curtains in the room. While starting slowly, once the flames began to catch, the two curtains burned like paper.

The mistress wished she had a moment to admire her work, and maybe continue her snack, but the fire was growing. Instead, she quickly reached into the cigar box, took a handful of cigars, and stuffed them into a pocket of

15

her jacket. She jerked her head in surprise when a fire alarm started sounding. Valentine took this as her cue to leave and headed out the door.

The other person confused by the sound coming up out of nowhere was the woman with cat ears in the room with Jon. She was about to ask what the sound was when Jon silenced her with a finger.

Jon walked softly to the wall with the entryway in it. He motioned for the woman to step back. The reason was very apparent within a few seconds. The guard who had stood between the entryway and Caine smashed through the door while flying backward. His body skid across the floor and came to rest when he bumped up against the vanity. The kimono from earlier slid off and covered him where he remained, motionless.

"What's going on?" Caine asked, entering through the broken door. "People started rushing by and out, but that guard stayed put."

"Sounds like a fire alarm," Jon surmised as he shrugged.

"Yup," Valentine tapped the big guy on the shoulder to get him to make room and stepped around him. "I started it. This her?"

"Figured that much." Jon nodded at the woman who began checking the motionless, yet still breathing, body of the guard. "You're covered in blood. You ok?"

"Don't worry, Jon," The woman stood up, now armed with a pistol. She checked to make sure it had a round in the chamber. She handed the weapon to Jon and gave him a violently toothy grin. "It's not mine."

"Tell me you were attacked first, Alegra." Caine's tone soured.

"Sure. Why not?" Alegra Valentine patted the suited man on the chest. "Now, can we get out of here before we all catch fire?"

"Why is the place on fire?" Caine continued the questioning as the group followed Alegra out the door. Jon made sure to check all the doors that he could from the hallway. Although he was slowing the group down, something in him had to make sure everyone was out.

"I saw enough," Jon informed his big friend as they continued. "So, I texted Alegra and called an audible."

"Yup," Alegra agreed, holding the group up as she peered through a doorway to investigate the main. "Jon called an audible and got to save someone. I had a snack and set a building on fire. You even got to punch someone. Everyone is happy."

"I kicked him." Caine corrected her. He looked back to make sure the woman they had rescued was still with them. Her gray tail had poofed up and her eyes had grown large.

The main room was empty as the group entered. The smell of smoke had gotten stronger as they moved. That scent told the four that the fire had caught hold of more and more as time went on. It was just as strong when they reached the outside.

A few of the guards stood outside watching the place burn but quickly turned their attention to the foursome as soon as they came out of the building. Two newcomers, one woman covered in blood, and a "worker" trying to leave with them. It did not take a wise man for them to realize that they were about to be picked as the culprits of this whole incident. The sound of their weapon's readying solidified this.

"We're just going to get in our car and leave." Jon made his way out in front of the crowd with his hands up. "We didn't find this place. We were never here."

A gun went off and Alegra hit the ground.

"Fucker," The woman groaned as she got to her feet. A wicked, toothy grin crossed the half of her lips that remained. She spit out a few teeth through the new hole in her cheek. "Bullets really fucking hurt."

The guards stood frozen; none of them able to comprehend what they were seeing.

"Excuse me, ma'am," Jon turned to the woman with the cat ears. "Can you come with me? We are going to find some cover. It's about to get rather messy out here."

The woman could not have followed the command even if she wanted to. Her body was locked in place as she witnessed the woman who was just shot, being thrown by the tall, scary man who was with them. He had thrown her straight at the guards before them and she latched onto one of them, driving her teeth into the side of his face.

Jon grabbed the cat-eared woman and ushered her behind a car. Her look was almost catatonic as she continued to try to comprehend this turn of events, and what they meant as the two rushed over to a car in the parking lot and ducked down. Jon pulled out his wallet and found a small piece of paper with names scribbled on the front.

"Whose turn is it?" Jon ran his finger down the page. "Here we go. Ma'am, you are about to see me do some weird things. Don't be frightened. Remember, I'm here to help you, but right now I need to help my friends. Ok?"

The woman silently nodded.

"Great," Jon smiled. "Oh man, how rude of me. I never introduced myself. I'm Jon. Jonathan Bringer. You are?"

"I...mew...I..." The woman meowed a pitiful, scared meow. A gunshot rang out again, followed by a few more.

18

"We'll do introductions later." Jon sat down on the ground and took a deep breath. "Spirit's within me, hear my call. I am the captor, you are the prisoner. I ask a favor. Upon completion, I will grant your release. Who will come forth?"

Slowly a mist began to form. The woman felt her ears go back instinctively. Jon's concentration was not even broken when a guard flew over the car and into the grass. The guard attempted to get back up when a black flash pinned him to the ground. Soon the man was screaming and twitching.

"Fucking noses..." Alegra spit the man's nose on the ground before going down for another bite; eventually, the man stopped moving. Alegra then vaulted over the car and back to the battle.

The shapeless figured floated in front of the two. A soft voice spoke. While quiet, it was still loud enough to fill the ex-prostitute's thoughts. That was when she realized the voice was not external, it was in her head. She also realized that while it sounded like words, not a single recognizable syllable filled her thoughts. Every fiber of her being told the woman with cat-like features to run. Run fast.

"Ah, Alec," Jon greeted the figure before him. "There is a body soon without a soul on the ground there. Take control of it and help my friends in their fight. Fulfill this request and you will be granted your freedom."

There were no sounds this time. The top of the gray figure simply nodded.

"Excellent." Jon remained motionless as the mist moved from in front of the two and enveloped the lifeless body. Soon, the feet began to twitch, followed by fingers; then, after some twists and jerks, the body began to bring itself to its feet. The body continued to jerk and shuffle as it joined the melee and fired off a few rounds from its weapon and into the people it once may have considered friends.

The "friendly fire" caused cries of confusion and panic amongst the guards. That panic and fear lead to silence a few moments later.

"All clear," Caine called out.

Jon gently grabbed the woman he was escorting's arm and brought her to her feet. He helped her over to the car that Caine and Alegra had already climbed in. Jon opened the door and gestured for the woman to get in. After all she had seen, she figured it was best for her to do as she was told. Jon climbed in after her and shut the door. Before their seat belts were even buckled, Caine slammed the car into gear and the group sped off into the night.

Chapter 3

"Damn," Megan Fairchilde muttered as she tapped her debit card on the counter of the university coffee shop. "Let me try that again. Maybe it didn't read it right."

"Ma'am," the barista started to look annoyed. "You've tried it three times. Payment has been declined each time. Tell you what. There is a line forming behind you, and this is the cheapest drink in the place next to water. I'll just pay the dollar ninety-five for you to move things along. Ok?"

"Thank you." The girl with dark purple hair sheepishly smiled as she took her drink. "Sorry, I just moved into town for class and haven't found a job yet."

"You were here last year and had the same problem. If it helps, we have a board over there where anyone can post anything," The barista instructed as she pointed to the corner. "Maybe you can find something there."

"You have got to be my guardian angel," Megan beamed and walked over to the board. "Thanks."

The board was covered in many laminated and hand-written postings. Looking over the ads, Megan absently took a drink and found it too hot. She cursed herself for not letting it cool and continued to look.

Ads to sell books. She had her books.

Ads to go see local bands. She took note of a few dates and kept looking.

A small ad written on notebook paper caught her eye.

Help wanted: See Dr. Jon Bringer. A few dollar signs were drawn on the paper.

"Jon Bringer?" Megan read out loud as she pulled down the ad. She took her backpack off and opened a pocket to pull out her class schedule. "I have him as a professor this year. That'll be an easy four point if I get a gig with him."

Megan tossed the ad in her bag.

"Ma'am," the barista called to Megan. "Can you please put that back up? So, others can see it too?"

"Keeps the competition down." Megan began to leave.

Megan arrived at class at a few minutes early, hoping to get a chance to speak with this professor. However, she found that she was the only one there early. Having a choice of seats, Megan elected to find one next to an electrical outlet; she used it to plug in a laptop she brought to help take notes.

Slowly, a few more people began to trickle in. Eventually, the room filled up. Except for a seat next to Megan. Finally, a disheveled looking man rushed in and took that seat. He placed a beat-up backpack on the ground. He began to dig through the bag to pull out a notebook. He continued his search through the bag but cursed softly under his breath when he came back out of it pencil-less.

"I'm sorry." The man adjusted his glasses as he turned to Megan. "I forgot a pen. Could I borrow one?"

"Yeah, sure," Megan responded and began digging through her bag, found one and handed it to him.

"Thank you," The man clicked it a wrote a few scribbles to make sure it worked. "The instructor show up yet?"

"No," Megan checked her watch. The class would have started by now if the instructor had shown up. Megan began to wonder if her future employer was always this tardy and if he would excuse her being late for work.

"Great." The man leaned back. "I heard this is such a blow-off class. The professor only shows up about half the time. Figured it would help my GPA. Guess I was right, huh?"

"I was kind of looking forward to it being pretty in-depth." Megan looked around and noticed a few people were checking their watches too.

"Really?" The man turned to face her more comfortably.

"One, I'm paying to be here and want my money's worth." Megan tapped her fingers on the desk. The tardiness of the professor began to grate on her more and more. "Two, Cryptozoology has always fascinated me."

"What got you into it?" The man began to pay no mind to everyone else in the room. One person began to gather their things and left the room. Megan thought it was a little too early to think the instructor wasn't showing up, but she didn't figure it was her place to say anything.

"I watch a lot of ghost shows and stuff like that." Megan felt a little embarrassed admitting that.

" You mean the ones," The man's interest perked up, "where they constantly go 'Did you hear that?'"

"Yeah," Megan's annoyed tone shown through as she didn't think too keenly of the mockery. "Those."

"They're total bullshit." The man looked as a few more people left. "Lot of post-production and why are all the ghosts from the eighteen hundred's? I just once want one where the only EVP they get is of the ghost going 'WHHAAATTSSSUUPPP!'"

"So, you know a little about ghost hunting," Megan crossed her arms. "Knowing what an EVP is and all that."

"I mean..." The man scratched his head. "I guess I should get up and teach class, huh?"

"Huh?" Megan was caught off guard.

"Sorry for the wait, ladies and gentlemen." The disheveled man got to the front of the class. He walked over to the door that the people had been leaving from, motioned for them to return, and when they did he made sure it was closed.

"My name is Dr. Jonathan Bringer, and you all just passed your first quiz for my class. In the world of cryptozoology, patience is a virtue," Jon continued. "You may not see what you are looking for at first, but if you keep looking and, like the young lady I took a seat next to, listening to clues, you can find what you are looking for."

Jon walked back to the seat he had taken next to Megan and grabbed his bag. He dug through it and pulled out a stack of papers. He began to pass out handfuls of the papers to the students in the front and made sure they began to trickle back to the rest of the class.

"A little information about myself," Jon began. "I am a doctor in parapsychology. I have authored a few books. They have all been total flops, so I am still teaching. I have also been on hundreds of encounters with spectral inhabitants, or ghosts. I have even investigated bigfoot sightings. Never been to Loch Ness tough."

A student raised his hand, and Jon pointed at him and nodded for him to go ahead.

24

"You've seen a bigfoot?" The young student asked.

"About the only thing I haven't encountered are aliens, the Loch Ness monster, or a bigfoot," Jon admitted. "Ok, I've mainly encountered many, many inhabitants. Way too many of them. I tend to focus on the dead and undead."

Jon stood at a whiteboard and drew a little cute ghost. Then he drew a cute little vampire.

He heard a student scoff slightly. It was a normal sound for the first day of class. Jon had gotten used to it over the years. These students lived in a world where the supernatural was a fantastical thought to them.

"The paper in front of you is the syllabus." Jon changed the subject. "You can see there is a lot of page numbers listed. Those are the pages for the textbook. The nature of my research means I tend to do a lot of late-night work. So, there are plenty of days I won't make it in. If the reading is done, you should be fine. I won't put anything on the tests that isn't in the book. Frankly, I just use these class sessions to expand on what is in there and tell a few personal stories."

Another hand went up. Jon called on the student while moving to sit on the corner of a table in the front of the room.

"Are you telling us ghosts and things like that are real?" the student asked.

"Some sightings are genuine," Jon explained. "Some are fictitious, like what you usually see on TV. Most are somewhere in the middle of the story. That's why we study cryptozoology. To better understand the sightings and understand the evidence that is all around us. To help us discern between fact and fiction."

"Then why are they treated like they aren't?" Another student piped in, continuing their line of questioning.

"A few reasons," Jon rubbed the stubble on his chin. "A great example is what I refer to as inhabitants. They inhabit a specific place. Your typical house ghosts. There is a ton of actual scientific research being done. However, a bunch of people with a camera and an editing program is what gets viewers, so that is what gets on TV. Yeti sightings are in that same category. There is plenty of good evidence, but a few rednecks with beer guts and a monkey suit get the airtime. So, people tend to lean towards those explanations. Another reason is predatory. Guess what, humans? Not the top of the food chain. Those things that tend to eat people like to stay hidden and not believed in. It makes it easier to hunt. Lucky for us, those things are so few and far between they are hardly ever noticed."

A small vibration came from Jon's pocket. He pulled out his cell phone, hit a button and put it back in his backpack. Jon tapped his foot a bit and buried his chin between his thumb and forefinger. He scratched his head and stood up.

"On that note," Jon announced. "Since introductions are done, go ahead and read the chapter assigned. We will be discussing it during the next class. Until then, I know this was short, but class is dismissed."

The class wasted no time in packing up their things and leaving. Everyone aside from Megan that is. She packed up her things and approached the desk in the front of the room where Jon had sat down; he was busily pressing buttons on his phone and did not seem to notice her approach. Jon sat there for a minute silently. He then put the phone down, grabbed a pen and wrote some notes.

Megan could not help but feel a little disappointed. She had expected things to be a little more drawn out and for class to be longer than the few minutes it had lasted. She figured it would be best not to question it as she approached Jon.

"Excuse me," Megan tried not to interrupt Jon too much. "Dr. Bringer?"

"Yes?" Jon set the pen down and smiled at his student. Megan couldn't help but feel genuine warmth from it. "Oh, the ghost show girl. I'm sorry, I didn't even ask your name."

"Megan," Megan shot her hand out, which Jon shook. "Megan Fairchilde."

"Nice to actually meet you, Megan," Jon leaned back in the chair.

"Same," Megan dug the ad from the coffee shop out of her bag and showed it to Jon. "I wanted to talk to you if I could about this ad from the coffee place. About you needing help."

"People actually looked at this." Jon took the ad and chuckled a bit.

"I was wondering what the job would entail." Megan stood up straight and tried to make herself look a little more impressive than she felt.

"A research assistant," Jon informed her. "I do a lot of field research and don't always have time to look into things properly. Teaching, being on the field, searching for missing persons; it gets hard to juggle it all. So, I'm looking into getting an assistant."

"I can do research." Megan nodded understanding. "I mean, I wrote enough papers to get me this far in life."

Jon got a good laugh out of that.

"Alright," Jon agreed with her line of thinking. "It might be a little more involved than that. I also do a lot of my research in the field, so I'll need you there with me."

"I'll get to go on crypto hunts with you?" Megan squeaked, but tried to hide her excitement.

"And get paid on salary instead of hourly," Jon added. "Since I might need you to research something at any time."

"I still get to go out on the field with you?" Megan beamed.

"How about a field interview?" Jon looked at his notes from earlier. "See how it all happens. If you don't get too freaked out, it sounds to me like you got the job."

"When do we go?" Megan was glowing. She had always wanted to go out on a ghost hunt and now was her chance.

"Tomorrow," Jon informed her. "That call was from a colleague of mine. A human-focused psychologist. Said she got a call about a young child developing schizophrenia, and that something about her didn't feel right. She wanted me to look before she makes a final diagnosis. You might want to pack an overnight bag or something. We could be there quite a while, depending on the situation."

"Will do," Megan pulled out her phone. "I'll give you my number so we can meet up."

"Sounds good, Megan," Jon could not help but share her excitement. "I look forward to working with you."

Chapter 4

Alegra Valentine groaned as she slowly got out of bed. The alarm had gone off three times now. However, she had found the snooze button too enticing not to hit. Plus, the mattress, had made the pain from the night before just a little more bearable.

She searched through her dresser for a bartending outfit and put it in the bathroom the night before. Sleepily, she started the shower, checked out the damage on her body. The bullet holes in her chest had healed enough to not even leave scars. Her face was a different story. The side of her mouth that was missing lips and a small chunk of her jaw had returned but a nasty scar now covered it.

After her shower, she changed into the clothes she left on the toilet seat. A little bit of makeup for the day, and to try and conceal the facial damage, left her disappointed with the results. She threw on a fake, black respirator, to hide it further. She finished her outfit and decided to head to work.

Opening a door that looked like a closet entrance in her living room revealed a staircase down to the floor below her apartment.

The door at the bottom lead to an office, with just a simple desk and laptop. After flipping a few switches, the lights came to life and it was time to get to work.

Alegra went to the main barroom and started with counting out her till for night. Satisfied with how much in change was in the register, she turned to the bar. With a quick wipe of a rag all the prep work for the evening was complete. She thought for a second about plugging in the jukebox, but she had grown so tired of all the music on it that she decided to leave it off, hanging an "out of order" sign on it.

The locks on the shutter on the front door made a heavy click as she slid them out of place. She reached down and put a key in the padlock that was holding a shutter to the floor. Then, with a quick lift, the shutter rolled itself up into the ceiling.

"Evening," a muscular looking woman greeted Alegra with a wave from the other side of the glass entryway.

"I know, Whit," Alegra moaned as she blocked the incoming light from the low hanging sun from her eyes. "I'm up late. I opened late. You know the routine. You were here, you'll get paid."

"I wasn't going to say anything about that." Whit shook her head as she stepped inside the small hallway leading to the bar proper. "Hell, figured you had a rough night or something and would be up eventually. Your apartment is upstairs. It's not like you have far to go."

"Spent the evening with Jon and Caine," Alegra confessed as the two made their way into the bar. Whit took her jacket off and hung it on a rack in the office.

"Ouch," Whit gave her sympathies as sat down at the bar. "Does sound like a rough night. What were you and the professor up to?"

"Ehhh…" Alegra frowned behind the mask as she made the disappointed noise and poured a shot of whiskey for Whit. Alegra always figured that putting a drink in her bouncer made her ready for any trouble. Not that Whit had ever backed down from a fight or problem in the place. "Went to a strip club, made some money to keep the lights on here, stole a nice hat from their wardrobe and knocked out the club owner when he got too handsy. Then lost the hat somewhere."

"And you didn't invite me?" Whit faked disappointment and downed her drink.

"Think about the company," Alegra reminded her. "Besides, I was the best looking one there and you would have gotten bored of looking at me."

"Nope," Whit shook her head, making her brown shoulder-length hair bounce and smiled. "Part of the reason I still work here."

"Sexual harassment against your boss?" Caine's voice broke up the conversation as he ducked into the room. The same black suit from the night before still adorned his tall frame.

"Someone in this place has got to make me feel a little special." Alegra shrugged turning to the door. "It's why I keep her around. Encourages me to go to the gym and keep in shape. Can't disappoint my biggest fan, now can I?"

Caine made his way past Whit and stopped at a stool next to her. He took the jacket of his suit off and put it on the back of the chair behind him before sitting down. He leaned back as he looked at the tap handles from behind his sunglasses, pointed at one and waited for Alegra to pour the beer for him.

"How's our friend?" Caine asked as he took his first sip.

"Refuses to eat." Alegra leaned on the back counter. "I also think she's terrified of me. She hissed and tried to scratch me earlier."

"Smart cat." Caine began to look towards the door as if he was expecting something.

"You got a cat?" Whit asked getting up from her seat.

"Jon found a stray last night." Alegra took the empty glass and cleaned it out. "Guess who gets stuck with it."

"Aww..." Whit gave a small laugh. "Guy has a heart of gold. He could do wonders for a demon like you."

"Get to work, Whit," Alegra scowled at the teasing. "Why does everyone suggest that?"

"Alright," Whit stood up and headed towards her stool just inside the door. "Going to work, boss. I know, I know, trading a client for a boyfriend would cut into your bottom line."

"Jon's a client of yours?" Caine asked raising a hairless eyebrow above his glasses.

"No," Alegra tossed the idea out of Caine's head. "That would be weird. It just usually shuts her up and stops her from asking questions."

"Fair enough." Caine took a drink. He looked back towards the door and noticed Whit had stuck her nose in a book that she had picked up from her stool. "Has she said anything?"

"Have you heard her?" Alegra scoffed. "She almost constantly runs her mouth. It's like having an older sister that is always taking the piss out of me."

"No," Caine took another drink. "The cat."

"Sorry." Alegra leaned closer so the two could talk without being heard. "Poor girl is still terrified. She was quiet all night, but whenever I would get close to her she

32

would turn white, hiss and scratch at me. She was so scared she pissed on the carpet when I tried to give her a sandwich."

"Do you think she saw you when you killed the guy trying to get behind the car?" Caine brought up the earlier encounter.

"I dunno." Alegra turned and started to put the beer one Caine's tab. "Jon said he was going to come over tomorrow night and try to talk to her. So, unless something comes up, I'm going to have to deal with her until then."

"And if something does come up?" Caine smiled already knowing the answer.

"I'm going to drop her off at his apartment with a note," Alegra joked. "Or an animal shelter."

The two shared a light chuckle as they heard Whit ask someone for their ID. It was time to get the night going.

Chapter 5

The Sun had just begun to set when Megan arrived at the address Jon had given her. She wondered what people thought about her standing outside of the beautiful suburban home, alone. Were they going to call the cops on her saying she was scoping out the place? She wished she had asked to ride with her professor, but she was too enthralled with the idea of finally having some sort of job that that thought had not even occurred to her.

    Luckily, she did not have long to wait as a simple looking car pulled into the driveway. The engine turned off and out stepped Jon. This time the disheveled professor was replaced with a neat and trim looking man in a well-tailored suit. He then walked to the other side of the car and opened the passenger door to pull out a briefcase and a notebook.

    "Hey," Megan greeted and approached her new employer with a warm smile. "I guess this is the right place."

    "Oh!" Jon gave a bit of a jump. He had not been expecting her to beat him there. "Sorry. Did I keep you waiting? Had to go pick up some equipment."

""Just got here a few minutes ago." Megan told the man as he closed the door and the two made their way to the front door. "The bus was a little early."

"Should have offered you a ride." Jon knocked on the door and pulled out his wallet. He removed a business card and kept it in his hand.

"No worries," Megan shrugged. "Bus dropped me off just a little bit from here. A little walk never hurt anyone."

Their exchange was interrupted as the door was opened by a woman in her late twenties. A look of confusion crossed her face as she took the two in. One being a well-dressed man, looking ready for a board meeting; the other being a purple-haired woman with too many piercings in her ears who had been staked outside of her house for the past ten minutes.

"Hello," Jon greeted the woman with a toothy smile and held up his business card like a badge. "I'm Dr. Jonathon Bringer and this is my assistant Megan. We spoke on the phone about your consultation with a colleague of mine, Dr. Waytes?"

"Yes." The woman's look of confusion faded as she opened the screen door. "Come on in."

"Thank you." Jon took the door from the lady and held it open for Megan.

The inside was immaculate as the outside. A large TV sat in the living room where the group was led. There were sounds of a child somewhere in the house playing, and the furniture that adorned the room most likely had not been sat on in quite some. Everything was also the color white; everywhere. The paint on the walls and the carpet were all white.

Jon sat down on the sofa adjacent to the coffee table and set his briefcase on the floor between himself and

Megan. The woman sat in a chair next to the two of them but still turned to face the TV. Megan wondered if the room was more for entertaining and there was a separate room for the family to relax after a hard day at the office.

"Thank you for making a trip on such short notice." The woman looked to let her guard down and gave an exasperated sigh.

"Well," Jon leaned in closer to the woman as if to reassure her that everything would be alright. "When it comes to mental issues with young children, the sooner we can diagnose the issue the sooner the treatment can become a normal part of their lives."

"That's what I don't understand," The woman admitted her lack of understanding. "Dr. Waytes said she would prefer your opinion before making a diagnosis."

"She is very cautious about certain mental conditions," Jon informed the woman whom he assumed was the child's mother. He opened the notebook to a page with simple, and basic information and pulled out a pen from his jacket. "Schizophrenia is a serious condition that can be hard to diagnose in young children. It could be something simple as an imaginary friend or an overactive imagination. That's why she called on me for my opinion. She said your child's name was Tina. Did she ask Tina all sorts of questions?"

"She did," the woman nodded, "but she didn't spend as much time with her as I would have expected. She came out of Tina's room very shortly after going in. I don't know how much time she would have really had to talk to her."

"I see." Jon wrote something in the notebook. "You told Dr. Waytes Tina hears things? What does she hear? Also, could you give me an idea when she said she hears them?"

"When exactly she hears them," the mother leaned back having heard all these questions before. "I couldn't tell you. She says every now and then, but they're getting more and more frequent. As for what she hears…"

"Sorry to interrupt." Jon scribbled more notes. "Can you tell me when they started?"

"Recently?" The mother thought back for the answer. "She never really talked about when they started."

"How old is Tina?" Jon scribbled again.

"Five," the mother tried to peer over at the notebook. "She'll be six in June."

"Great," Jon lowered the notebook so the woman could see it better. He did not want to come off as hiding something from the fretting mother. "Did Dr. Waytes talk more to you than her?"

"Yes," The mother nodded.

"Ok," Jon wrote again. "One more important question. It's just voices. No visual hallucinations?"

"Nothing she has ever mentioned." The mother was satisfied with what was being written down.

"What time is Tina's bedtime?" Jon set the notebook on his lap.

"Eight," the mother informed him starting to feel more comfortable.

"I see." Jon tapped the pen on the notebook. "There would be no reason for her to be up in the very late of the night."

"Doctor," The mother's voice started to show less concern. "What are you thinking?"

"That talking to Tina might be our best option right now." Jon handed the notebook to Megan.

"I'll go get her." The mother started to get up.

"Is she in her room playing?" Jon stood up. "If so, I would like to talk to her there. That way she can be more comfortable."

"Sure." The mother led the two to the stairway and upstairs.

The child's room was a beautiful sky blue with a dollhouse and various toys spread all over. A lone child sat in the middle of the floor playing with plastic building blocks.

"Tina," the mother called to the child to get her attention. "This is Dr. Bringer and his assistant. They want to ask you some questions about the voices you've been hearing."

"Hi, Tina." Jon sat on the floor with the child. "You can call me Jon. What are you building there?"

"I dunno." The child quietly responded.

"Can Megan and I play too?" Jon asked and motioned for Megan to come and sit with him.

"Yeah." The child looked to her mother for guidance about the stranger. The mother nodded in approval.

"Great." Jon smiled, adjusted his glasses, and he began building with the blocks. "How long has it been since you played with these, Megan?"

"I was always terrible at building with them." Megan reminisced and began to connect blocks together.

"That is the magic of them," Jon corrected her as he did the same. "No matter how bad you are, whatever you build is always amazing to you."

"I guess." Megan vaguely agreed.

"So, Tina," Jon looked to the young child with hair like her mother's, "how old are you?"

"Five." Tina looked over at what Megan was building. "That piece should go there."

"Sorry," Megan laughed.

"Is okay." The child continued.

"Do you have a lot of friends at school?" Jon continued to build.

"Yeah." Tina nodded.

"Good," Jon continued with the child. "You play with them a lot?"

"Yeah," Tina confirmed as she connected more blocks together.

"Do you go to visit their house?" Jon asked reaching for a blue block. "Do you have fun over there?"

"Uh-huh," Tina confirmed.

"Do you hear the voices there?" Jon asked not taking his eyes from what he was building.

"No." Tina put her blocks down.

"Only here?" Jon tried to confirm but did not want to lead the child. "Nowhere else?"

"Yeah," Tina said as she stopped playing. She then got up and grabbed a plastic fashion doll. "She sounds like her."

"Like her?" Jon took the doll. "Not scary?"

"She sounds sad," the girl told him. "She asks me to help her."

"Well," Jon smiled a big smile and leaned in close to the girl. "What do you say we help her?"

"You know how?" The little girl's eye lit up.

"I have a very good feeling I do." Jon reassured the child. "Now I need to go talk to your mommy really quick. You and Megan have fun. If you hear the voice, I need you to tell her, ok? Megan, if she says she hears the voice, come get me."

Jon approached the mother and gently led her out of the room. The two made their way to the hallway and Jon closed the door behind them.

40

"I have good news," Jon began. "I don't believe Tina has schizophrenia. Dr. Waytes did the right thing by having you call me."

"So, what's she hearing?" the mother asked hurrying for an answer.

"Do you have any history of this house?" Jon asked. "Any previous owners?"

"Just an old man," the mother started filling in details. "I don't remember his name."

"That's fine," Jon led the mother back down the stairs. "You see, Dr. Waytes and I have worked together for years on cases like this. There is no easy way or even a believable way to put this. I am not just a psychologist. I specialize in parapsychology. I believe your home may be inhabited, haunted in a more laymen's term."

"What?" The mother's response was as flat as Jon had heard a million times before.

"Your house has an inhabitant." Jon casually informed her. "A ghost. Usually, when a schizophrenic voice is heard, studies show that in Americans it is usually malevolent. Due to the description your daughter gave, it didn't sound that way at all."

"What?" The mother was not believing what she was hearing.

"Don't worry." Jon put his hands up as he reassured her. "She just seems lost. I can take care of this for you. If you want me to."

"You're shitting me." The mother finally broke her line of questioning. "This is a scam."

"Afraid not," Jon scratched his head, "and it's not a scam. I have no interest in even charging you for the removal. Is your husband home?"

"No, he's at work." The housewife shook her head. Jon could not tell which unnerving her more. Was it the

41

thought that her house was haunted, or was it that he was asking what might be too personal questions?

"Ok," Jon mused as he rubbed his chin in thought.

"Why?" The woman grew concerned.

"I don't want to scare, Tina," Jon informed her. "I believe the spirit may be weak and can only talk to Tina due to her age. Children have a much more open mind about these things, so it doesn't take as much energy to make contact through them. I'm trying to think of a way to do a removal, without upsetting her."

"Look," the mother's expression continued to sour as she interrupted Jon's train of thought, "you have no proof. You're probably going to tell me to take her elsewhere and then the two of you are going to rob us blind."

"That's why I was thinking your husband could be here," Jon explained as held his hands up in defense. "I can prove it. I have my equipment. I have something called a spirit box. What it does is it scans radio waves to create white noise and help the spirits speak through it. Why don't we have Tina go in the other room and watch cartoons or something? You and I will use the box in her room. If you're not convinced, we'll leave and call Dr. Waytes to come in as soon as she can. Sound good?"

The mother threw her hands up. Jon wasn't sure if it was in frustration or defeat. Either way, she silently nodded, and Jon couldn't help but let out a big grin. The mother walked back into the room. After what sounded like a brief conversation, the mother led her child out and downstairs. Jon followed them and grabbed his briefcase. He returned to the room with the mother and she sat down on the child's bed.

Jon opened the briefcase and pulled out a small electronic box and set it in the middle of the room. Megan watched over Jon's shoulder as he fiddled with the buttons.

The box started making noise and sounded like a radio flipping through channels quickly. Jon leaned on the dresser and folded his arms, listening intently. Megan had not moved from her position, nor had she breathed. Jon reached over and tapped her on the shoulder, which caused her to jump. With a smile, he made a few deep breathes and Megan emulated him.

It was only a few more minutes when the group got what they were listening for. The box made a noise sounding vaguely like the word "Help."

"Bingo!" Jon exclaimed as he shot up. "I just heard a cry for help. Did you hear it, Megan?"

"I don't believe it." Megan eeked out.

"Oh my god." The mother put her hand over her mouth stunned.

"So," Jon began, proud of himself, as he turned off the box quickly and tucked it back in his briefcase. "Believe me now?"

"Is it dangerous?" The mother quickly asked.

"I wouldn't assume so." Jon put his hand on the mother's shoulder to steady and comfort her.

"I don't care." The woman shot up from the bed flustered. "I want it out of my house."

"I can do that," Jon sat down, "but I'm going to need the two of you to leave. Like I stated before, I don't want to scare Tina."

"How long do you need?" the mother asked, "and how much is this going to cost me?"

"A few hours," Jon figured. "I'm not going to charge you. I am a paranormal researcher. To me, this is all research. Just allow me to use this case as a teaching study for my classes. I'm sure they would love to hear about this."

"When can you start?" The mother now more relieved started to head to the door.

"Right now." Jon smiled. Jon motioned for Megan to escort the mother out the door. After both shook off the stun from what they had just witnessed, she did so. After a few minutes, Megan returned to the room.

"What the fuck..." Megan was in a slight state of shock. "I just heard a fucking ghost."

"You didn't hear the inhabitant of this place." Jon rejected her idea. "Like I told you in class, those ghost shows are simply parlor tricks and aftereffects."

"I know what I heard." Megan's voice rose as she felt she was about to be verbally attacked again.

"What you heard was a yelp noise," Jon explained as move some of the toys around and make an open space in the floor. "The box flips through the nearby stations at a very rapid pace. Eventually, you are going to hear something that sounds like a word. Usually, how it is explained is that it only goes through dead channels, but it's a dumb device. It has no idea what is making a sound or not. As soon as I heard something, I quickly jumped on it to plant the idea of what the sound was in your head."

"What?" Megan deadpanly responded.

"Because I'm the professional," Jon's smile was a cocky as he sounded, "you all trusted me. What you heard was whatever radio station that little box picked up, or it was a mixture of two when it hit something in between live stations. All I needed was that sound to convince you both."

"Why would you pull something like that?" Megan crossed her arms.

"I knew the place was haunted as soon as I walked in." Jon began to gently touch the walls of the room. "I felt the energy of the inhabitant. It's weak, but I could feel it. I needed to make sure the child was in no danger, so I talked to her and asked what the voice was. Since she said the voice was female and needed help, I could assume she was safe.

That was the only way to make sure if the mother didn't believe me."

"How did that doctor know to call you?" Megan was slowly becoming fascinated, watching the man closely. "How could you feel it?"

"Dr. Waytes specializes in schizophrenia and felt the child did not fit the description of the typical sufferer. She's been an old friend of mine for ages, and I have accompanied her to these things before. Took a bit to convince her too. So, she and I have done this song and dance since for quite some time." Jon tapped a spot on the wall and sat on the ground facing it.

"But how did you feel it?" Megan asked looking where Jon was staring.

"That's a very long story," Jon shut his eyes concentrating. "The truly short version is I'm a necromancer. Now, I need to concentrate. The spirit's energy is telling me that it is a bit older. It will take a bit more for me to draw them out."

Jon sat motionless for a bit. Megan could not tell how long. She was transfixed as her new employer continued to stare straight ahead as the dark of night began to take over the room. After what seemed like an eternity to Megan, Jon slowly reached his arm out. Then, after making a few precise movements with his fingers, he turned his hand over, leaving the palm face up. Slowly, a greyish light began to glow around his hand. Megan had never seen a light like it. The light had no illumination of its own, but the grey aura was clearly visible in the dark.

Within moments, a column of gray fog, that had a color to match the one in Jon's hand, emerged from the wall. The fog, which stood maybe five feet tall, began to grow and take shape; a nude female shape.

45

"There you are." Jon lowered his hand and smiled politely.

"Oh my…" Megan gasped softly and hid her mouth behind her hand. Jon held a finger up to silence his assistant.

The figure moved its mouth, but no sound came out.

"My name is Jonathan Bringer," Jon introduced himself as he stood up and moved over to the figure. "I'm here to help you, but I need you to speak to me. I need you to find the strength to talk to me. Try very hard."

The figure moved its mouth. Nothing came out. Jon kept motioning to encourage the figure.

"He…" The figure finally let out. Megan could not explain it. There was no actual sound coming from the ghost. It was all in her head.

"Yes." Jon grinned like an idiot as he looked at his assistant's continued stunned expression.

"Help…" The figure continued.

"Yes," Jon moved closer to the figure, "I'm here to help you. The family here would like you to leave. I need to know why you can't. I want to help you move on so everyone here, as well as you, can be at peace."

"No peace…" The voice rasped, and the figure shot back away from Jon, leaving an after image of the figure.

"Why?" Jon quizzically rubbed his chin.

"Scared… lost…" The figure continued as it looked around the room. "Searching."

"Oh," Jon nodded solemnly. "I think I understand. What are you scared of?"

The figure did not say anything. It was frozen in space.

"She's weak," Jon scratched his head trying to find the best course of action that he needed next, "Let's try this. Make motions as well. Ever play charades in life?"

"Alone." The figure responded and pointed down.

46

"What does that mean?" Megan softly asked.

"It could mean a whole lot of things," Jon pointed out. "From experience, my best guess is she's afraid of the other side. Something happened in her life to make her believe that she wouldn't be going to a good place in the afterlife. However, the word 'alone' is usually not accompanied by that gesture. Usually, the fear is something dark or violent. Torture is a good example. Sadly, that leaves me with one option."

"And that is?" Megan asked.

"Are you scared of Hell?" Jon asked and the figured nodded in response. Each movement leaving a grey trail of light.

"How about we make a deal?" Jon had finally come up with a plan. You said you were searching for something. I can help you find that. While we search, you can come with me. However, there is a catch. In return for coming with me, and us searching for whatever it is you are looking for, you will owe me a service. It can be a big world-changing ordeal, or it could be as simple as getting me a cup of coffee. How does that sound?"

The figure tilted its head left and right in thought.

"Megan," Jon did not turn his gaze from the spirit. "I need you to find the bathroom here. I may need it here very soon. This part is always hard on me. If the deal gets made, I need you to grab my notebook and whatever I say, I need you to write down. Ok?"

Jon could not see Megan agree. His quick instructions snapped his assistant from her trance.

"Accepted." The figure spoke.

"Great." Jon held his hand out gently to the spirit.

The grey glow grew again from his hands. The figure slowly reached out and touched Jon's glowing hand. Then, slowly, the spirit moved into Jon and when the two became

47

one, the spirit disappeared. Jon's eyes grew big and he dropped to his knees. He looked around quickly and reached for a plastic wastebasket.

"Oh God." Jon began to gag, and eventually threw up into the basket. He made a scribble motion with his hand. "She's a lot stronger than I thought. She's young. Helen. No, Ellen. Ellen Chandler. Born 1920."

Megan began to write as Jon vomited again in the wastebasket.

"Died 1946 by... oh God, Ellen. Suicide. Husband, Vincent Chandler, never..." Another vomiting fit ensued. Jon spat mucus and saliva as the contents of his stomach were sufficiently empty. "Never returned from the war. She never got a Dear John letter or a letter of his death."

Jon sat back as his body calmed down. Sweat coated him and his face was beat red even in the darkness. A deep breath escaped him, letting out a small gray light. His tired eyes shifted over to Megan who was just finishing up the notes she was taking. Jon pulled out a handkerchief and wiped his mouth. He sat back against a dresser, and he slid the bucket away from himself. Jon gave a thumbs up showing he was ok.

"That was real," Megan eeked out. "That was a real ghost."

"That was a real ghost...inhabitant." Jon emitted an exhausted laugh at his new assistant's amazing look. He reached his hand out for her to help him up which she did willingly. "Usually, unless they're older, I don't get that sick."

Jon found the restroom and cleaned out the bucket he used.

"Starting tomorrow," Jon washed his hands in the sink, "I need you to start looking into what happened to Ellen's husband. I keep my promises to people."

48

"I can start tonight" Megan agreed. "I don't think I can sleep after all that."

"Then what do you say we have a drink to celebrate your new job?" Jon patted his new employee on the shoulder.

"I'm not old enough to drink," Megan turned down the offer. "I'm only nineteen."

"I know a place that will let you in." Jon sat down in the house's living room and shut his eyes. "Head on over there. I'll wait for these guys to get back and then head over. It's called Misshapen. The bouncer gives you any trouble, tell her you're with me. She'll let you in. Also, just a bit of advice about that place. Try not to stare."

Chapter 6

For being a college town, New Hancock did still have its share of places one would rather not be at night. Since Megan had moved to town last year, she had heard rumors of where they were, and she made it a point not to avoid them. Megan had even heard rumors of a bar in one of the rougher neighborhoods that was run by the son of a neo-Nazi. At the same time, she had heard that it was one of the safest places to be. However, the location of Misshapen was not in that safe neighborhood.

Megan looked around the area after she got off the bus and found the bar she was looking for; a dark storefront with all the windows blocked out. Having moved here from Chicago, she was much more used to the brightly lit bars of the Wicker Park area with their large open windows and loud party scene. Misshapen was about the opposite of this. There was one window that was boarded up and the rest had a very dark tint that did not allow anyone to see inside. All Megan could even see as she walked up to the glass of the front door was a bored woman slogging her way through a thick romance novel.

Megan hoped to herself that her new employer was right and that if she name drops him, she would be let inside. The door scraped along the ground as Megan pushed it open.

"ID." The woman did not even look up from her book.

"Umm…" Megan began to dig into her back pocket for her wallet. She pulled out her ID and gave it to the woman who held her hand out. She handed the piece of plastic to the bouncer. The woman just lazily fumbled it around in her fingers and handed it back to the girl without ever looking up from her book.

"Enjoy." The bouncer greeted Megan as she motioned the girl to move further into the bar.

The inside looked as run down as the outside, but almost as if that were the décor design the establishment was going for. The main bar counter was nicked and dinged with large sections of mismatched varnish and stain. The wall opposite it had a raised platform, which Megan guessed was a stage for live bands to play. However, the dust and cobwebs said it had not been used in at least a decade. Other than that, there were a few tables with chairs and a more modern and sleeker-looking jukebox on the wall that was unplugged. Various mirror advertisements and neon lights continued with the dive bar vibe.

The place was empty aside from two patrons and the bartender. A woman, who was dressed in a grunge fashion that looked a few decades out of date, was doing her best to ignore the tall, bald man sitting next to her. Even from the distance, Megan could see him chatting away at her. The woman was not the least bit interested. Megan ignored the two and found a seat at the bar.

She did her best to shy away from the bartender in hopes that the woman working the counter would ignore the fact that she looked underage. She had told herself to find a table and just wait for Jon. However, avoiding wanting to look at the bartender was impossible for Megan.

Megan had never seen a person like this before. It was not the fact that the woman was heavily tattooed, or how revealing the outfit she had on was. It was the fact that she had two horns protruding from the top of her head. Each horn stemmed from opposites sides of her forehead and curved towards the back, along her temples. One was mangled and damaged; looking like it could break off at any second. The other was much shorter and did not even make it back to her long, bright red hair. It appeared that it was starting to grow back into her skin.

"Welcome to Misshapen." The bartender smiled seductively, showing a set of almost too-perfect teeth. That smile was almost as captivating as her golden, shimmering eyes. "I'm your new Mistress: Mistress Valentine. I'll be taking very good care of you this evening. So, what can I start you with?"

"I'm..." Megan was so captivated she could not make out words.

"Or," the woman leaned closer on the counter, "are you here for something else? Don't worry. I don't discriminate based on sex. I do have various prices depending on your tastes."

"I think I may have come to the wrong place..." Megan squeaked out.

"Alegra," The tall man stopped talking to the other woman and turned his attention to the two. "I think your new patron is a little nervous. You're coming off a bit strong. Right?"

Megan just slightly nodded.

"See?" The tall man chastised the bartender. "Besides, she looks underage. You might want to talk to your bouncer."

"What?" The bartender's tone changed to a much more flat and disappointed tone. "Seriously? Let me see your ID."

Megan pulled the ID back out and handed it to the bartender. The horned woman read it, put her hand on her forehead and handed it back to Megan.

"Sorry, kid," the bartender apologized. "I need to ask you to leave. You have to be 21 to drink here."

"I'm sorry," Megan took the ID back. "I was…"

Megan tried to explain when the bartender just walked away and made her way to the bouncer. Megan couldn't hear what was being said, but she figured it wasn't good.

"Strange." The tall man in the black suit turned to Megan, and he motioned for her to take a seat next to him. It was at this time she couldn't help staring at his man too. Not a single hair adorned his head. No mustache, not even an eyebrow, not even a hint of a five o'clock shadow. Looking even closer, Megan noticed something even more curious. He had no lips; they were simply painted on with lipstick. Black mirrored sunglasses hid his eyes. At this point, Megan just hoped there were eyes underneath. "Whit is usually pretty good at checking IDs. Wonder why she let you in?"

"No idea." Despite the strange appearance of the tall man. Megan felt more comfortable talking to the man in the suit. His friendly yet awkward smile just made her feel more at ease, and his tall frame made her feel safer. She chose to follow his instructions and take a seat. "I was told by my new boss to meet him here and if I said his name, I wouldn't have any problems."

"Really?" The man sipped on his drink. A bit of his lipstick came off on the rim. The man used a napkin to wipe the smudge off. "What's his name?"

"Jon Bringer," Megan answered hoping it might do something. It did. The man let out a strong, almost inhuman laugh.

"Seriously?" The man tried to confirm the information. "Are you his research assistant?"

"Yeah?" Megan was not sure if this was a good thing or not.

"Alegra!" The man called out. "Get your ass back in here. You owe me a bottle!"

"What are you yelling about?" The bartender returned in a huff.

"Meet Jon's new assistant." The man presented Megan.

"You fuckin' serious?" The bartender, apparently named Alegra, cocked an eyebrow.

"Yes?" Megan again felt unsure. "Jon told me to meet him here."

"Fucking A…" Alegra threw her hands up. "Alright Caine, what do you want?"

"That bottle of vodka has been staring at me since we made this bet." The tall man pointed a finger, without any knuckle cresses, at a bottle on the wall.

"Come on." The woman threw her hands up. "That is top-shelf shit."

"Bet's a bet." The man raised his glass as the bartender reached up and pulled the bottle down. Now, feeling slightly more comfortable through the jesting of the two, Megan was able to take notice of something she had only caught a glimpse of when the bartender left. A strange, fleshy looking lump covered by a large scar stuck out of the woman's back by her left shoulder blade. The lump appeared to move independently of her shoulder. The same spot by the right shoulder blade had a scar, though it was almost unnoticeable due to a large tattoo.

"Excuse me," Megan interrupted. "Is everything alright?"

"Alegra bet me Jon would never hire anyone," The tall man, who was named Caine grinned as he eyed the bottle now in his hands. "She said he never would listen to her ideas."

"I've known him for about twenty years." Alegra placed her hands on the counter. "Now he listens to me. Sorry, kid, didn't know you were with Jon."

"Sorry, I should have said something." Megan tried to smile as she found herself being more and more comfortable with her new company.

It was at this time a familiar face made his way through the door and took a seat next to Megan. Jon was dressed in a normal t-shirt and blue jeans and had obviously showered.

"I don't even want to speak to you," Alegra greeted Jon and turned back to the shelf trying to make it look like she had not just removed a full bottle from there.

"Hey." Caine raised his victory bottle at Jon.

"I see you are already making friends," Jon smiled at Megan and gently patted her on the back. "Don't understand how Caine got his hands on that bottle though."

"Something to do with a bet." Megan brought Jon up to speed.

"What were you guys betting on?" Jon asked as Alegra brought him a beer without him ever asking for one.

"If you would listen to Alegra and hire an assistant," Caine informed him as he reached over the counter for shot glasses. Alegra slapped his hand back and brought them out herself.

"Why?" Jon looked confused. "I take advice."

"When was the last time you took mine?" Alegra put her hands on her hips.

"I've taken it plenty of times," Jon protested.

"Name once," Alegra leaned closer to him. Jon stopped and thought for a second. Alegra then stood up straight and pointed a finger at Jon. "Do not answer that."

"Fair enough." Jon relented the point as Caine poured a shot for everyone, including Megan. He offered one to the woman he was talking to earlier, but she refused. Caine then stood up, and placed it in front of the uninterested lady again, and took one to the bouncer. The woman still did not take the drink, she just pulled some cash out of her pocket, tossed it on the counter, and left. Alegra scooped it up and began to count the change for the woman, completely missing that she had walked out the door.

"To Jon," Caine toasted as he raised his glass. Everyone took the shot, aside from Alegra, who threw it over her shoulder. "Who actually listened to good advice."

"A bartender that doesn't drink?" Megan wondered out loud.

"It's a little more complicated than that." Jon straightened himself after the shot. "Let me introduce you around. Tall guy is Caine Grimm. The name sounds like it came from an edgy sixteen-year-old. We are all fully aware of that. Fell free to make fun of him for it. The bouncer is Whit. She's cool. Our lovely hostess for the evening is Alegra Valentine. Stripper, bartender, dominatrix and actual demon."

"Demon?" Megan tensed up.

"Horns didn't give it away?" Alegra teased as she began to clean out the mini glasses.

57

"I…" Megan did not know what to say. The fact that a demon now stood in front of her just mesmerized her. "I thought they were a prop?"

"Don't feel bad, everyone does." Alegra waved off the apology. "First time you met something supernatural?"

Megan looked over to Jon, unsure of how to answer. She was not sure if she had offended Alegra or if it was a legitimate question. Jon just nodded at her and motioned for her to say whatever she was thinking.

"Sorry," Megan apologized quietly. "I didn't mean to offend you, but yeah this is the first time."

"Oh sweetie," Alegra gave an understanding smile. "You didn't. I've gotten used to that a long time ago. At least you didn't walk in here and tell me Halloween is over."

"Also, she's not your first." Jon corrected Megan from behind his drink.

"Oh!" Megan got excited. "I saw an… inhabitant?"

Caine almost spit out some of his beer with a quick chuckle.

"For fuck's sake," Alegra groaned. "He's got you saying that kind of stuff? Betcha also went on and on about how all the ghost shows on TV are fake and how they do it. He always gets his feathers in a mess over that."

Jon rolled his eyes.

"They're ghosts, Jon. You talk to ghosts." Alegra walked back to the tip jar after realizing the patron left. Afterward, she replaced Caine's drink and turned to Megan. "He ever tries to get you to call me anything other than a demon, hit him. You have my permission, and if he fires you for it. I'm calling in his tab."

"I'm just trying…" Jon began to defend himself.

"Jon," Caine reached a long arm behind Megan and touched Jon on the shoulder. "Let it go. Just let it go."

"Speaking of names," Alegra finally turned her attention to Jon. "I think you need to find out the name of your new pet. She won't eat, and just kind of sits in the corner of the room and hisses as I walk by. Tried to scratch me once. Want to go up and see her?"

"Sure." Jon finished his beer and stood up. Megan looked around making sure he was talking to her, then stood up to follow him. "Ready to go see something else?"

"Go ahead." Alegra grabbed a set of keys from next to the cash register and tossed them at Jon. "We're slow so I'm going to get the tall drunk out of here and close up shop. I'll be up there in a bit."

"You just gave me a fresh one," Caine protested as Jon and Megan got up.

"We're in a college town," Megan could hear Alegra instruct Caine. "Chug like a frat boy."

Chapter 7

"We'll go up the back," Jon instructed. "I don't want to drag dirt on her carpet. I'll never hear the end of it."

Jon and Megan left the bar and walked around to the side of the building, down an alley and past a few dumpsters to a rickety wooden staircase. Without hesitation, Jon made his way up the stairs while flipping through the keys Alegra had handed him. Megan looked around and took a step on the stairs; she hesitated, sure that her and Jon's weight would collapse the staircase. When she was certain it would hold both their weight, Megan followed Jon.

Jon held the door open for Megan as she stepped inside. Jon slipped off his shoes in the dark room and switched on the light to the tiny apartment. Megan also took hers off, and the two stepped further in the room. It was painted a pristine white and had a brown carpet held down place by a small couch. A respectable sized TV sat opposite it, its blank screen reflecting the contents of the small space. Megan felt a strong desire to explore the demon's apartment, but she knew to wait for Jon to do something first. After all, this did seem like familiar territory to him.

Jon set the keys on the counter in the kitchen, which was connected to the living room. He turned to make sure the door was closed behind him.

"Is there anyone here?" Jon called out and began to walk around the apartment. "Hello?"

Megan waited in the living room. She was still slightly in awe. She was just a normal college kid looking for a job a day ago, and now? Now she had seen a ghost and watched her employer "absorb" it. As for right now, she was just casually standing in a demon's living room and was feeling, disappointed? She did not know what to expect, but a normal apartment was not it. No black candles, no satanic imagery, nothing. Just a normal TV with some action and a few rom-com DVDs and that was about it. Megan was just waiting for a cat to show up any second. It would probably be a grey tabby named "Tiger" or something.

"There you are," Megan could hear Jon greet warmly. "It's alright. You remember me, right?"

Megan followed the sound of his voice to the other room to find Jon crouched down; he was talking to what appeared to be a woman dressed in pajama pants and a band t-shirt. She was crouched down in front of Jon, hiding by the bed and looked terrified.

"Oh my god," Megan gasped. "She's a demon and she kidnapped someone!"

"Shhh..." Jon quickly turned to Megan and hushed her.

"Kind of," Alegra's voice came from behind Megan. "Kidnapping her was Jon's idea."

"We rescued her." Jon held his hand out to the terrified woman. Megan could not understand why, but the woman shied away, hissed softly and then sniffed his hand.

She couldn't pinpoint it, but something was off about her nose. After that, something perked up on the top of her head, splitting her hair. Two soft cat ears twitched as they unflatten themselves.

"What on earth?" Megan softly asked.

"It's alright," Jon continued to talk to the woman who seemed to be warming up to him. "We're not going to hurt you."

Alegra excused herself as she slipped by Megan to walk to the dresser opposite Jon and the cat woman. The cat woman quickly turned to her and hissed loudly, and then jumped in front of Jon as if to protect him.

"Yeah, yeah." Alegra paid the cat lady no mind and grabbed a change of clothes from the dresser. She then returned to the other room to presumably change. "You're big and tough."

"You're scared of her?" Jon asked in a soothing tone.

"She's dangerous." The woman explained her actions to Jon as she kept her eyes on the door. "You saved me, so I'll protect you."

"That's Alegra," Jon told her. "She helped me save you. She's our friend."

"She is?" The woman put a finger to her chin and stared up, obviously confused.

"Of course, she is," Jon reassured her. Alegra returned to the room, and Jon stood up and put his hand on Alegra's shoulder. Alegra nonchalantly took Jon's hand and let it drop to his side. "She's kind of a bitch, but she's nice. This over here is Megan and she's a good person, too."

The woman crawled over to Megan and sniffed her. Then, with a smile, rubbed her cheek against her leg. Megan held her hands up defensively, confused by what was going on around her.

"She didn't act like this at the strip club..." Jon pondered to himself.

"Masters would hit me if I didn't act like people." The woman explained.

"Makes sense," Jon nodded understandingly. "No one would want to sleep with a cat, let alone a nekomata. So, if she acted human..."

"Professor?" Megan chimed in, interrupting his train of thought. "I am still kind of new at this. What's a nekomata?"

"You're looking at one," Jon smile began as if class was in session. "They're a type of Japanese yokai or spirit. The story goes when a cat becomes incredibly old it becomes a nekomata."

"I'm not old!" The nekomata was offended at this implied statement. Her tail, which Megan had just noticed and had to reconfirm for herself the woman had, got straight and her ears shot back. Alegra took this as her opportunity to get away from everyone learning about the yokai and go to the kitchen.

"Sorry," Jon apologized. "I didn't mean it like that. But I was just stating that in Japanese folklore when a cat gets rather old..."

"You're not making it any better, Jon," Alegra called from the kitchen which was punctuated by the sound of a closing fridge door. "So, drop it."

"I'm just explaining..." Jon said, trying to defend himself.

"Anyone hungry?" Alegra called out changing the subject.

"I could use..." Megan started.

"You don't want anything," Jon informed her.

"Why?" Megan questioned.

"You just don't." Jon continued and turned his back to the doorway to take a closer look at the nekomata. Just then, a hard and cold object bounced off his back.

"It's fucking ham, asshole," Alegra snapped at Jon. "I can't eat this shit, and your cat isn't, so I was nice enough to offer you a sandwich. Megan, would you like a sandwich made of ham and bread. I may even have some mayonnaise in here."

"Why are we making such an effort to say it's ham?" Megan questioned.

"She's a demon," Jon informed her, hoping Megan's mind could fill in the blank.

"Not following." Megan's confusion punctuated her words.

"I'm a demon, kid," Alegra pulled a white package out of the fridge and poked at it to see if it was thawed. "I don't eat human food. Makes me sick."

"So," Megan walked into the kitchen with the ham projectile in hand. "Are you a vegetarian?"

Alegra dropped her head to the side with a slight laugh. She then nodded slightly and stuck her fingers in her mouth. With a quick pull, she removed her top and lower sets of "teeth" and placed them on the table. In place of the two neat nice rows Megan had seen earlier, two rows of pointed, jagged and sharp teeth now glistened at her.

"These teeth ain't for plants." Alegra opened the white package which held a hunk of meat inside. She then pulled out a pan and sprayed it down; after this, she put it on the stove and turned on a burner. Her voice changed to a more hushed tone. It was as if the voice became slightly ashamed. "I'm a demon. I eat flesh. Human flesh. Sorry, am I starting to scare you?"

"Truthfully?" Megan looked around. She still felt unsure but was starting to realize that despite all the

65

weirdness going on around her she was very safe. It appeared that everything was in control. "Out of everything I've seen today, you're probably the most fascinating one."

Alegra let out a sharp laugh as she opened the cupboard and pulled out a loaf of bread.

"You hear that, Jon?" Alegra called out as Jon and the nekomata left the bedroom. "Your new employee says I'm cooler than you."

"She also doesn't know you," Jon sounded slightly jealous. "You said she hasn't eaten yet. Since we all trust each other, maybe we can try having her eat again."

"I'm not hungry." The nekomata shook her head. "I mean I was, but then when you showed up and I felt all well and good and warm."

"I see." Jon nodded not knowing at all what that meant. "You know what? You seem to have calmed down since we picked you up the other day. Why don't we get to know each other a little better? You seem to remember me. I'm Jon."

"Alegra," Alegra introduced herself to the creature now that she was no longer afraid of the horned woman.

"You were there to rescue me too?" The woman said. Her cat eyes got big and shiny as she gazed at the horned woman.

The yokai got up and slowly walked over to Alegra. She gave her a few quick sniffs and then butted her head against the horned woman's shoulder. Alegra's eyes showed confusion as the woman then began to nuzzle her. She mouthed *what do I do?* to Jon who just shrugged and motioned for Alegra to pet her. Slowly, Alegra did just that.

"Oh my god…" Alegra smiled. "She's purring. Jon, she's fucking purring."

"Did you help *meow* too?" The nekomata moved over to Megan and looked up at her. Alegra tired to hide her look of disappointment by going back to her meal.

"No." Megan shook her head. "I just started working for this guy. I'm Megan."

"Yay!" The creature cheered, hugged, and began to rub on her too. "More friends!"

"Umm…" Megan went quiet again. "Can…can I pet you too?"

"Please," the woman begged. "I need all the head pats."

Megan began to rub the woman's head too. No one was sure which one of the two quietly giggled, but both seemed to be enjoying themselves.

"What's your name?" Jon asked, not trying to interrupt what he guessed was the woman's first moments of happiness in an awfully long time.

"My old master used to call me, Cat Bitch." The cat got deep into thought. "So, I think it's that. Nyan."

Jon shook his head.

"No," Jon corrected her line of thinking. "Before you were brought there. Surely, you had a name before that."

"Before that?" The woman cocked her head thinking hard. "I don't remember a 'before that'."

"Probably forgot," Jon guessed. "She's had a lot of trauma, and that could cause disassociation. That will lead to chunks of memory missing as she blocks out the world. Mind if we call you something else until you remember?"

"I get a name?" The woman started to get excited. "Can I get a pretty collar too?"

"I got you covered on that," Alegra got up and left the room for her bedroom. She returned with a wine collared velvet collar and tried to give it to the woman. The woman looked at it and gave it back, only to present her neck.

Alegra, getting the message, buckled it on her. "My ex-husband gave me this a while back. You can have it."

"It's so pretty!" The yokai jumped up with glee. "It's so soft too!"

"Guess we got to think of a name." Jon couldn't help share the joy and happy excitement that came from their new friend.

"We can call her Mittens," Alegra chimed in.

"She's a person," Jon shot back, almost offended. "Or a sentient being. Not a cat."

"How about Miko?" Megan suggested. "She looks like a cat character I saw in a video game. She would always end her sentences with something that sounded like that in the Japanese voices."

"I like Miko," The newly dubbed Miko cheered with a toothy grin. "I have a name!"

"Alright," Jon began to head to the door. "Miko it is. Well, it's early in the morning and I've had a long night, and I'm sure someone has classes in the morning. Why don't we call it all here? Miko, are you ok spending another night with Alegra?"

"Can I sleep on your bed?" Miko looked to Alegra with wide, hopeful eyes.

"I'd really rather you didn't." Alegra shook the idea off.

"Ohhh..." Miko groaned in disappointment. "Please?"

Miko gave Alegra puppy dog eyes in hopes that she would change her mind.

"Don't give me that look." Alegra looked over at the assault of cute eyes. "Cat, we don't even know each other well enough for you to be doing that... Fine! Just don't hog the bed."

"Yay!" Miko exclaimed again.

"I think that settles it," Jon walked to the door and put his shoes back on as Megan followed suit. "Miko can stay here until we can figure out who she originally belonged to before she became a nekomata. Then, we'll find your family and return you home."

"Good night, everyone," Megan spoke up as she followed Jon out the door. "It was good meeting you all."

"Don't be a stranger now, kid," Alegra held the door as they left. "And good luck with him."

After they left, Alegra finished her meal, washed her dish and headed towards the bedroom, shutting off lights as she went. Miko excitedly pranced into the bedroom behind her.

Chapter 8

After the exciting night, Megan's morning came way too quickly. She had hit the snooze button on her phone's alarm clock three alarms ago. Finally, the young woman rolled out of bed with a groan as she realized it was not going to accept a delay for the fourth time.

"I'm moving," Megan told the device as she finally hit the dismiss button. She did not want to be late for classes. Before she re-enrolled, she would have just ignored it and she would have made up some excuse not to go into the fast-food job she had that was barely keeping the bills paid. She knew she was trying to start a future for herself by going back to school to finish her degree. Messing around on that was not something she wanted to do for future Megan.

Looking around, she could see she was alone in her dorm room. She figured her roommate had gone to start her day already. When they first met, her roommate had told her that she was an early bird and usually went running in the morning. Megan was amazed she didn't hear her roommate's alarm go off but then realized that she had probably slept through it.

She went into the bathroom, washed her face, and brushed her teeth. After that, she returned to the tiny dorm room. She grabbed fresh clothes from her dresser and changed out of her PJs. She checked her phone for the time as she hurried out the door. She would have to skip breakfast as usual.

The student body of the university was already much more alive than she felt. She checked the phone's clock again and found she had a little extra time before her class. Jon's office was in a building next to where her class was and so she decided to stop off.

She pulled out her syllabus to make sure she was headed to the right floor and quickly found the door with Jon's name on it. She gave a quick knock, but she was slightly disappointed when there was no response.

"Was wondering if you might show up," Jon's voice came from behind her. Megan turned to find the professor walking up behind her with two paper cups of coffee in a drink carrier. "So, I grabbed you a cup too. It was a late night."

"Thank God." Megan took the drink carrier so Jon could unlock the door.

"And early morning coffee shops." Jon held the door open to a tiny room with a messy desk, and two chairs; one on either side of the messy desk. Megan stepped inside, taking in the various degrees hung upon the wall.

"How did you know I would come here first?" Megan took the seat across from Jon and took a sip from the coffee with an "M" scribbled on it.

"Before I got into teaching, I initially wanted to be a psychologist." Jon took the other and put his feet up on what looked like the only clear spot on the desk. "So, I spent way too many hours in classrooms learning how people think; enough to be a doctor. People are very predictable, and when they see new and strange things, they usually feel they need some sort of validation. The first person they would probably go to seek that validation from would be the person who appears to know what is going on. In your case, you came face to face with a lot of the supernatural last night. So, naturally, I guessed you would go to the man leading you through it. I figured it would be a phone call or a visit. If it was a phone call, then both these cups would be mine."

"So," Megan summed it up for herself. "You either look like a nice thoughtful guy or got two cups of coffee."

"Winner either way," Jon concluded.

"I thought your doctorate was in parapsychology." Megan leaned back.

"Do you honestly think," Jon took his feet down, "a reputable college is going to give someone a doctorate in supernatural beings? That was just a passion project that got turned into a career. You pull a string here, you publish a few things there and boom, they let you teach it. Not for a lot of money, mind you, but it's steady work. It funds my other projects."

"Other projects like Miko," Megan confirmed to herself.

"That's the short version of it," Jon agreed to Megan's line of thought. "Anyway, I'm glad you're here. Do you still have those notes you took when I was throwing up?"

"Yeah," Megan did not bring them with her. "On my desk in my dorm, I think."

"Great," Jon sipped his drink. "I need you to look into that information. I need you to find out all you can about that woman's husband. She wouldn't let me sleep last night. She wanted to make sure I remembered my promise."

"I thought you like dispelled her," Megan leaned in closer, "or sent her away or something."

"No," Jon shook his head. "I wish. I took her into me. Easy way to explain it is that I let her haunt me. There's more to it, but that's for another day. Necromancer stuff. You probably have a class soon. I'll explain another time."

"Ok." Megan stood up. Jon was right, her classes were about to begin soon, and she made a promise to herself to be a better student. "Do you need me for anything else tonight?"

"Just to look into that for me." Jon reconfirmed his instructions. "I have a few things to do tonight. We'll talk more tomorrow after class. Maybe go over to Alegra's and you can play with Miko some. She seems to like you two ladies. She must be feeling rather good to finally have friends."

"Tomorrow then." Megan stood up and headed to the door, drink in hand. "Thanks again. If I find out anything, I'll let you know."

"That's what I pay you for." Jon waved as Megan left.

The hallways were empty as Megan walked through them. She pressed the button for the elevator to take her back down. She waited and waited, checking her phone for the time. If it got there quickly, she would be just in time for her class. However, her impatience got the better of her. Stairs were healthier anyway.

As she dropped down the stairs, she could hear two voices. Two guys sounded like they were discussing an arson that had been on the news recently.

"Heard the strip joint off of 73 burned down," one of them said to the other. "Friend of mine that works there said three people came in and burned the place down. He said the chick with them had horns."

74

"The fuck you mean horns?" The other guy laughed off what he was told. "Like a costume or some shit?"

Megan slowed her decent. When she got close, she hid behind a corner. Stripper with horns. She knew someone like that.

"Naw," the first guy elaborated, "like real ones. Said she was a new dancer. Said she was a real smoke show too, blonde, tatted all over and just had a dominating presence about her."

Could not be who Megan thought it was. Alegra was a redhead.

"Damn," the second guy breathed lost in his imagination. "Wouldn't have minded seeing that. That place was a hottie freak show. She burn the place down?"

"Sounds like it," the first guy confirmed. "He knew the place was run by a gang. As he was running from the fire, he said hc could scc three people squaring off with the gang that ran the place. Heard gunshots, screaming, then a car peeling off into the night. Rumor is, he said, is they came to take that cat girl."

"Not this again," he second guy laughed. "Brad, man, how many times do I have to tell you. There is no such thing as a cat girl."

"My buddy showed me pictures," the one named Brad contested. "You've seen them."

"All I saw was a woman with cat ears on. You can buy them at any anime convention. Cosplayers wear them all the time." The second guy explained, exasperated.

"Speaking of," Brad changed the subject. "I got a new hentai for our gaming sessions. This one has a hermaphrodite and a futa chick fuck each other."

"Hey," Megan interjected herself. She was finally able to put faces with the voices. "Sorry to be eavesdropping. I heard something about a gaming session. Role-playing?"

"Yeah," The second guy nodded. He was tall and thin enough to look malnourished, unlike his friend, who Megan was quick to assume was Brad. Brad was heavy set; he looked like he needed a shave and smelled like he needed a shower. "We have a small gaming group."

"Nice," Megan nodded. "Looking for new members? I'm new in town and have been looking for a group to join."

"We are pretty deep in," Brad began to decline, "and we don't have time to train a new player."

"What are you playing?" Megan continued to press.

"Dude," the second guy scolded his friend, and turned to Megan. "We're playing Dungeon Lords and Heroes, third edition."

"Fuck that mainlined fourth edition shit," Megan added. She had heard her brother say that before about the game, and she hoped she was using it in the right context here. "If I show up with a character you think the Lord of the Dungeon will let me in?"

"I'm Andy," The thin guy reached a hand out towards her. "I am the Lord of the Dungeon. Give me your number and I'll text you the address."

"Cool," Megan grabbed her phone and exchanged numbers. Andy realized she was not going to shake his hand and tried to play it off like it was nothing and stick it in his pocket. He pulled out his phone and the two exchanged numbers. "I'm Megan. I guess I'll be seeing you guys later."

"Yeah," Brad and Andy began to walk off. Megan then heard Andy say to Brad under his breath. "See if you talk to women, you can get their numbers, and not spend so much jerking off to anime chicks with dicks."

"Whatever," Brad scoffed. "Two times the fun."

Megan watched the two walked off and wondered if she had made a big mistake. Either way, it sounded like there was a supernatural creature burning down businesses and she needed to contact Jon. She checked her phone, realized she was going to be late for class and figured she would contact him later.

Jon's phone buzzed silently as he made his way back to his office. After attempting to pull it out of his pocket, dropping it, and then recovering it, Jon was able to see who it was. Megan had sent him a rather long text message.

"Herd something that might interest you. 2 guys were talking about a strip club that burned down along the highway. said some woman with horns showed up that night. also something about a cat girl. alegra & miko?" Was what the message read. Jon considered himself lucky that Megan texted like a semi normal person.

"Any description?" Jon messaged back.

"Blonde and tattooed for the woman, nothing about the cat." Read a message that was shot back after a few seconds.

"Might be Miko. As for the horned woman, Allergen is a redhead. I'll talk to Caine about it. Don't worry about it and focus on finding our husband. No need for you to get involved in the Miko situation. Got that taken care of." Jon sent back.

"if it's Miko, I want to help! some gang is involved, and I don't want her hurt. she's sooooo cute." A message came back to Jon's phone, with a heart-eyed cat emoji.

"Don't worry about it. She's safe. Allergen has a good eye on her. I'll talk to Caine and see what's up. I'll update you if I hear anything." Jon realized the autocorrect butchering of Alegra's name after he sent the message. Then realized Megan knew who he was talking about. He sat back and set down his phone. It buzzed back. He did not want to pick it up as he figured the conversation was over. He had learned that was never a good choice and looked.

"ok" was all it read from Megan. Jon may not have had the best people skills, but he knew that a simple ok from a woman was never something he wanted to read. He rolled his eyes and set his phone back down.

Chapter 9

"Hey, kid," Alegra greeted Megan as she entered the bar. "Jon ain't here yet."

"That's ok," Megan set her bag down and took a seat at the bar. "Busy today?"

Megan was nervous about what would happen without Jon. Alegra did not appear to be the type to throw her out without him, however.

"If you call three guys who have only ordered one drink apiece busy." Alegra washed a glass. "Anything while you wait?"

"Actually," Megan began quietly. She was not sure if she should be asking about Miko in the open, so she leaned in close so that Alegra could hear her whisper. "Is Miko here? I was wondering if I could talk to her."

"Miko?" Alegra laughed slightly and pointed behind Megan to where Miko was happily cleaning a table in a French maid's outfit. "She insisted on coming down and helping me in the bar today."

"And you dressed her like that?" Megan questioned.

"She raided my closet," Alegra defended herself to the young woman. "Some guys like to be bossed around by the help. Rich guys like it behind their wives back."

"Jon wasn't kidding about the dominatrix thing, was he?" Megan took another look at the bartender.

"Girl's got to pay the bills," Alegra shrugged. "He wasn't kidding about the stripping either."

"Is that what the stage is for?" Megan kept an eye on Miko as she cleaned happily with her tail swishing back and forth. She cleaned her way to the three guys sitting at a table. Her ears dropped back as she approached them, and then she slinked away back to Alegra.

"Those guys keep staring at me, nyan," Miko whispered to Alegra.

"That's cause you look good, girl," Alegra winked at the cat. "Now go over there and work it like I told you. They'll tip big."

"And I then give that money to you? Right?" The nekomata's tone became drab.

"No," Alegra laughed slightly at the naivete of the woman. "You're working. You get to keep it."

Miko's ears perked back up as she almost pranced back to the table with the guys. She bowed down real deep, greeting them, and tried to take their order. They just shooed her off. Miko turned back to Alegra and looked sad. Alegra just shook her head and mouthed for Miko not to worry about it and walked off to the front entrance where Whit was sitting. Alegra said something to Whit, who nodded and set down her book. The bouncer then got up and talked to the three men and all three nodded in agreement to whatever was said.

"They give you any more of a problem, cat," Whit approached Miko and put a hand on her shoulder. "You let me know. I'll toss 'em all out on their asses."

Whit then walked back to her seat and picked her book back up.

"To answer your question," Alegra continued the conversation with Megan. "Kinda. When I took the place over, I wanted to start a show club that specialized in the artists that no one else wanted to hire. The punks, the misfits, the whole alt scene. Poets, burlesque, musicians, anything. Something empowering and something different."

Megan noticed Alegra got quiet and began to rub her arms as if she were comforting herself. Megan was not sure if it was over the lost dream, but this is when she noticed more of the Alegra's features that she had not noticed before.

Alegra's tattoos hid scars that adorned her arms from her wrists to her elbows. Each one no more than an inch in length, but they completely covered her. Megan could not help but wonder if her legs were the same way, and how she got them.

"Looks like you're on your way," Megan added to cheer Alegra up and pointed at Miko.

"Still need something to do with the stage." Alegra smiled a bit at the idea that Mike was, in a way, a step toward her goal.

The entrance doorbell ringing interrupted their conversation. In walked a tall, bald man in a pitch-black suit. Caine took a seat next to Megan and without a word, Alegra brought him a drink.

"Jon show up yet?" Caine asked after his first drink.

"Didn't know he was stopping by," Alegra leaned on the back counter, "until Meg stopped in."

"Megan," Megan corrected her.

"Until the kid stopped by," Alegra corrected herself.

81

"Jon said he wanted to talk to me. He told me it had something to do with angels," Caine explained.

"And I'm just here to talk to Miko," Megan explained again.

"You all need to start buying more to drink if you all are going to keep using my place as a club house." Alegra let out an annoyed groan as she pointed a finger back and forth between them both.

Jon was not too far behind the scolding the two were receiving.

"New employee?" Jon asked as he sat down at the bar.

"She insisted," Alegra shrugged. "Been waiting tables since we opened. Since those three are the only ones that have been in here tonight, she's only been washing tables."

Jon was about to say something to Megan when Caine got up and approached him.

"You wanted to talk?" Caine towered over Jon, "something about an angel sighting."

"Yeah." Jon took a drink of whatever Alegra had placed in front of him. "Miko, can you come with us? Caine and I want to talk to you about the angel sighting you mentioned."

"But, Master Jon," The woman stood proud and determined to stay. "I've got to make all the tips! Nyan!"

"We'll tip you for your time." Jon got a chuckle out of the nekomata's determination. "Alegra, can we use your office?"

"You know where it is." Alegra waved the three off, and once again she was alone with Megan.

"Angels?" Megan's question broke the silence after a few minutes.

"I'm a demon." Alegra pointed at her horns. "Is it so hard to believe angels exist?"

"Kind of funny," Megan got the point. "Out of the few times I've talked to you, I tend to forget what you are. You come off just as human as Jon or I do."

"Thanks, kid." Alegra stared at the floor trying to hide the fact that she was beaming. Megan would never have known such a smile could come from a demon. The moment was broken, though, when the three men approached the counter.

"Another round guys?" Alegra greeted them.

"You're Mistress Valentine." One of the strong men confirmed calmly. All three had to weigh in at least 250 pounds each and it all looked like pure muscle.

"Sorry." Alegra shook her head. She turned and reached for a card on the back counter. Time to give the speech she felt she had given so many times it felt robotic for her. "I don't do parties. There have been some incidences. I'm sure you understand. However, I'm more than happy to give a private dance at any of the clubs I'm performing at. Unless you are looking for my other services in which case here let me give my infor…"

"We're here on behalf of Maximillian Grool," The spokesman continued. One of the other two pulled a knife out, and the other a small club. Whit set down her book and stood up. Alegra subtly waved the woman to stand down, and she made a jabbing motion showing that they were armed. "You have some of his property."

"I have no idea who you are talking about." Alegra walked from behind the bar. "I am going to ask that all three of you to leave now."

Megan felt her heart rate quicken. She swallowed hard and tried to stare straight ahead at the wall of liquor ahead of her. She did not want to do anything to upset them.

A gentle hand touched her shoulder gently. Alegra's hand gave Megan a squeeze as if to reassure her that everything was under control.

"You dyed your hair." The one without the knife said as he slapped Alegra with an open palm. The strike pushed her away from Megan as Whit still held her position.

"Kid," Alegra stood up and collected herself. "Get behind the counter and keep your head down."

Megan did not have to be told twice as she quickly found cover behind the bar.

"Now," Alegra checked her lip to make sure she was not bleeding. She looked down at her clean hand, almost disappointed. "I asked you to leave. Now, I'm telling you. Get the fuck out of my bar."

A club tip into her solar plexus was her answer. Alegra hit the ground; hard and gasping for air. Whit didn't need a signal this time. Without hesitation, she ran at the men and threw a superman punch into the jaw of the unarmed attacker knocking him to the ground. Alegra tossed something behind the counter and as Megan reached for the small white objects, her eyes grew wide. In her hands were Alegra's dentures.

Alegra was on the ground on her hands and knees when a foot came swiftly for her rib cage. Alegra caught the foot and twisted to her back holding on, sending the large man on his back. Whit was quick with a boot to the guy's head, sending him into a daze. The kick might have been a lucky turn of events for him, as he barely realized he was now being straddled by the bartender. However, his daze turned to horror as he felt teeth drive into the meat of his neck. Then, with a quick pull, a mouthful of flesh was torn from his body. Blood began to pour out of the wound. The man struggled in vain to close the wound with his hands, but the blood continued to flow through his fingers and onto the dark hardwood floor.

The two other thugs went to help their friend. A quick knife in Alegra's ribs should have stopped the assault. However, they froze in horror as Alegra turned to them; the hunk of neck meat still in her mouth. Using her teeth to hold it, Alegra began to use her hands to tear the piece of flesh into smaller bits. She quickly swallowed the portion in her mouth, and then greedily chomped down on the handful of meat. It did not take much more for the attackers to turn tail and run out of the building.

The man on the ground continued to struggle to try to pull himself out from under the much smaller woman. With the thug weakened by fear and blood loss it was nothing for Alegra to clinch a claw-like hand around the face of the man. She shoved his head back, exposing the front of his bloodstained neck. Another bite came, this time much smaller and much more deliberate. It too was quickly swallowed. The man's eyes widened; a little from the pain, but more from the shock of the realization of what was happening to him. Alegra had begun to eat him while he was still alive.

A blood-soaked hand attempted to swat at the demon. Being too weak from blood loss was no concern. His body was running purely on instinct. His mind could barely comprehend that the crunching sound, which came with no pain, was the attacking hand losing fingers to the woman's jaws. A few seconds more and the man's body went limp and became a feast for the demon.

Megan had not heard the fight for a bit and decided to come out from behind the counter. Whit quickly rushed over to her to try to keep her behind the counter; it was too late.

Megan's eyes grew large and her mouth made a silent scream that only came out in a strangled gasp. Alegra turned to the sound, holding the bloody arm of the man; a chunk of his forearm still in her mouth. She swallowed and tried to speak but was silenced by the much more vocal and horrified scream from Megan. The bloody visage and the vile smell were too much for the research assistant's stomach to handle and the meal she had earlier escaped her stomach the same way it came in.

The scream had alerted Jon and Caine as they rushed into the room. Alegra had begun to move closer to Megan. Jon was unsure if she were going over to calm her, but a bloody demon getting closer to a terrified person would only lead to trouble. Without hesitation, he threw himself between Alegra and Megan. He crouched down to Alegra's level and put his hands on her shoulders to stop her.

Megan took this as her moment and scrambled to her feet. She steadied herself after slipping on her vomit and bolted out the front door. Alegra's eyes grew frightened as she realized what was wrong, and she fell back from her knees to a seated position. She turned quickly from the front door and tried to hide away from any prying eyes. Jon gently put his arm around her to comfort her and the bloody demon buried her face in his chest.

Caine stepped around the body of the thug. He looked out the front door of the bar, trying to find Megan but saw nothing. Whit came up behind him and closed the shutter to the bar.

"What happened?" Caine asked Whit.

"Those three guys started a fight," Whit informed him. "Two guys pulled weapons, and another hit her twice. I decked one. The one on the floor here tried to kick her while she was down. She grabbed him and went to town."

"Sounds like self-defense." Caine nodded decidedly.

"That knife in her ribs not prove it?" Whit pointed out the weapon. "It's on the cameras if you want to watch."

"I'll take your word for it," Caine replied as he walked over to Jon and Alegra. "She ok?"

"She'll be ok," Jon nodded still holding Alegra close. "Must have lost it in the moment. I guess seeing Megan must have brought her back."

"I've got to go after her," Caine emotionlessly looked over the carnage. "You three going to be alright with this mess?"

"We've got this," Jon confirmed. "I'm going to get her upstairs and calmed down. Whit and I will take care of the body after Alegra is comfortable."

"I'm ok," Alegra whispered as she pulled herself away from Jon and tried to stand. She wiped blood and tears from her face, leaving bloody streaks down her cheeks. "I'm ok. I can help. They attacked first, had weapons..."

"Relax," Caine pulled up a chair for Alegra and helped sit her down. He slipped a handkerchief out of his pocket and wiped away some of the bloody streaks. "Whit told me everything. He was fair game. You can enjoy your meal if you wish to continue."

"I'm sorry." Alegra looked away from Caine.

"No need." Caine shook his head. Caine did not say anything. He motioned to the knife so Jon could see what he was doing. Jon leaned in and let Alegra know that Caine was about to remove it. The woman braced herself and with a quick jerk Caine removed the weapon. Jon placed his hand over the wound until blood stopped dripping between his fingers. When he did the wound had already began to close.

"It's all part of my job," Caine reassured her. "I'm going after Megan to make sure she's alright. See who she has told and see how to deal with it. You lost yourself in an attempted robbery. It's alright."

"Please," Alegra began to ask for a favor. "Apologize to Megan for me. She shouldn't have seen that."

"I'm going to go take care of her," Caine informed Alegra. Her body got noticeably still at the news. "Don't worry. I'm not going to hurt her."

"Thank you." Alegra sighed.

Chapter 10

Caine climbed into an old gray sedan and started the engine. Jon had given him Megan's full name, but he did not have an address. That was of little concern to him though.

Caine pressed a blank spot on his phone and a new screen in pure white popped up. Caine adjusted his sunglasses and began pressing what looked like random spots on the blank screen. He then closed the application and turned on the phone's GPS directions. Using his long fingers, he poked in an address and waited for it to calculate the directions. When it finally gave began giving instructions, Caine pulled the car out of the parking lot and drove off.

A dorm building on the local university campus was where the directions had led him. Caine parked his car in an open handicapped spot and turned it off. He opened the door and stepped out of the vehicle. Caine adjusted his tie as he walked up the stone stairs and through the front doors to the lobby of the dormitory.

"Excuse me, sir?" A young lady at the front desk called for Caine's attention. "Visiting hours are over. I'm going to have to ask you to come back tomorrow."

"I'm law enforcement," Caine informed the woman.

"Ok," the woman did not seem phased. "Do you have a warrant or any other reason to be here?"

"I'm looking for Megan Fairchilde. She stays in this dorm, and I need to speak to her." The tall man continued in a monotone voice.

"Let me ask again…" the woman was about to repeat herself when Caine reached in his pocket and pulled out a badge with an ID card.

"FBI," Caine interrupted her. "I need to talk to her about something she saw tonight. I need to do this as soon as possible before the memories fade. I cannot come back tomorrow. You will take me to her now."

"I'm sorry, Agent." The young woman pulled out a piece of paper and wrote a number down. She then handed the paper to Caine. "This is her room number. She just ran through here a little bit ago. She looked messed up."

"Thank you." Caine took the paper and found his way to the elevator.

He pressed a button to open the door, and once inside, directed the elevator where to go. When the doors opened again, Caine stepped out to a hallway of identical doors with different numbers. He walked down the hall and found the door with the number that matched what was written on the paper.

Caine rapped his knuckles on the door and waited. After a few minutes, he did it again.

"If it's for me," Caine heard Megan's voice say from inside. "I'm not here."

"Don't worry," another female voice said back. "It might be the police. They'll figure out what you saw."

90

Caine adjusted his tie as he heard the locks on the door disengage. The door slowly creaked open and a young woman stood in the open doorway. She looked the tall man up and down. Then without taking her eyes off him, she stepped back into the room and closed the door behind her.

"Who was it?" Caine heard inside the door from Megan.

"I don't know," The roommate's voice responded. "It is most definitely not the cops."

"Fine," A few footsteps followed. "If you don't want to ask, I'll answer it."

This time the door opened, and Megan stood on the other side. She took a second to collect herself and finally addressed the man in front of her. Without hesitation, she quickly closed the door. It took a few more knocks for Megan to open the door again.

"What do you want, Caine?" Megan crossed her arms in front of her.

"We need to talk about what you saw," Caine responded flatly.

"No." Megan tried to close the door on him. Caine shot his hand out quickly between the door and the jamb. Megan tried with all her might to close it, but the hand pushed the door open.

"That was not a request." Caine stared down at her.

"Fine," Megan relented. She realized that refusing him was useless. "You probably would have just stood outside my door all night."

"Would not have been the first time I've done that." Caine boasted his determination.

Caine stepped aside and waited patiently outside the dorm room. Megan called back to her roommate that she was going back out. The roommate walked back to the door and took another look at Caine. This time the bald man smiled awkwardly at her and gave a little wave.

"What if the cops show up?" The roommate asked and looked Caine up and down.

"I'm pretty much them." Caine flipped out the same badge that he showed the girl at the desk. The roommate just nodded and walked back into the room and closed the door.

"I didn't know you're a cop." Megan pointed out.

"I'm not," Caine explained. "Not for humans, anyway. Come on, let's get something to eat. I'll explain more."

"After earlier," Megan rubbed her stomach gently. "I don't think I want to eat."

"Ice cream?" Caine suggested.

"Honestly," Megan found a small chuckle escape her. She was not sure if it was the fact that the man in the black suit had just completely ignored what she saw, or just how innocent his suggestion was. "That has got to be the most innocent thing I've dealt with lately."

The walk down to the car was completely silent. Caine politely held the car door open for the woman and shut it when he made sure she was in completely. Megan buckled her seat belt as she waited for Caine to get in and start the car. The tall man paused when he got in and messed with his phone a bit, touching a completely white screen as if he knew exactly what he was doing.

"That will take care of the police coming," Caine smiled at Megan as he put the phone down. Megan instantly lost all color to her face and reached for the door handle. She jiggled it open, and in her panic, forgot to undo her seat belt. Realizing that Caine had never once made a move to restrain her, she realized that she was in no danger and calmed down. She silently reached out and reclosed the door.

"Sorry," Caine apologized as he started the car and drove off, "I could have worded that better. I meant they aren't coming to question you about what you saw."

"Of course, they're not," Megan expressed this with a sound of defeat in her voice. "I'm amazed at how little that surprises me."

The two exchanged no further words as, much to Megan's cynical surprise, they pulled up to a rather busy ice cream parlor. Caine turned off the car and climbed out. Then he made his way over to the passenger side to let Megan out of the car. Caine motioned for her to lead the way into the parlor.

"I love this place," Caine leaned down as he talked to Megan. "Full service. Let's go find a seat."

Caine motioned for Megan to follow him to a seat after they entered. For a second, she thought about bolting out the door but realized how pointless that would have been. He had already found her once. She didn't doubt he could easily do it again.

Megan took a seat at a booth and Caine took the seat opposite her. A waitress quickly came along and brought them both glasses of water and two menus. Caine set his aside and Megan picked her up, and she took a drink of the water. She was using it both as a shield to protect herself from the gaze of her host, prolong any conversation, and as a way for her to take a few deep breaths to try and remain calm.

"The usual for you?" The waitress spoke to Caine who just gave an approving nod. "And for you, Miss?"

"Chocolate shake?" Megan wanted to sound stronger coming out, but her courage escaped her.

"I'll take care of the bill," Caine offered, wanting to reassure her that there was no trouble. "Anything else you want?"

"No," Megan declined the offer.

"Well, if you want another or something for the road," Caine offered again, "just say something before we leave. I'll get that for you too."

Megan finally took a second to breathe and told herself that one of two things were about to happen. This man was either smiling so much because he was about to get a new people suit, or because he was trying to make her feel at ease. Either way, the amount he did it, was unnervingly inhuman.

"I'm just going to ask you straight out," Megan started after the waitress walked away. "Am I going to die tonight?"

"What?!" Caine was genuinely taken aback by the suggestion. "What would give you that idea? I'm taking you for ice cream."

"That smile and suit make you look like the bad guy in a horror movie," Megan explained. "You also hang out with a necromancer and a demon who eats people. What else am I going to expect but to be fed to her to keep me silent."

"If Alegra ever, and I mean *EVER*, makes an attempt to hurt you in any way," Caine's voice turned to a more serious tone, "I need you to tell me right away. If you are ever in trouble or threatened by something you don't understand, you come and tell me right away."

"Huh?" That was not the response Megan was expecting from the tall man.

"Remember how your roommate asked if I was a cop?" Caine reminded Megan. "I'm not exactly a cop. I am the front lines between the supernatural and the human world. In Alegra's case, I'm much less her friend, and much more her parole officer."

"Her parole officer?" Megan repeated, her tone becoming more questioning.

94

"Yes." Caine leaned back. "Alegra had an incident roughly twenty years ago. I am to keep tabs on her, and make sure she doesn't step out of line again."

"Not sure if you noticed," Megan interjected. "I saw her eating a guy. He was still alive and barely fighting for his life as she had her damn teeth in his jugular."

Caine slid Megan's water closer to her as he noticed her getting visibly pale at the thought. Megan took a drink, and a deep breath and her color began to return.

"Let me ask you," Caine began, "and if I feel a threat is still there, I will go and take care of Alegra. Who started the fight?"

"The," Megan paused to choose her words carefully. She wanted to tell the truth, but deep down, she didn't want anything to happen to Alegra. "The guy she was eating. She told me to get behind the bar before there was too much wreckage."

"Sounds like the same story Whit told me," Caine confirmed for Megan. "Self-defense. She's allowed to neutralize a threat anyway she sees fit. Mess with the bull, and you get the horns type situations. It also sounds like she was trying to protect you."

"Yeah," in the craziness of the situation, that fact must have slipped Megan's mind. Right now, part of her was questioning how she reacted. "She did."

"She feels horrible for what you saw," Caine apologized for Alegra. "She sent me to make sure you are alright. All of us just want to make sure you are alright. It can be jarring watching a predator eat its prey, especially when that act makes you realize you're not actually on the top of the food chain."

"I guess." Megan gently spun the ice in her drink with her straw deep in thought. "Alegra really isn't human. I know I've only met her a few times, but it's so easy to forget that. I mean, hell, someone even married her at one point."

"Horns weren't a dead giveaway?" Caine laughed.

"I guess," Megan now took a long look at the man across from her. She caught herself rambling, and she took a minute to collect her thoughts. "I mean, I dunno. I just kind of looked past them. I have a ton of friends with too much shit in their face. Hell, I've seen so much weird shit the past 48 hours that I… I don't know what I'm thinking or where I'm going with this."

"That's alright," Caine reached out to pat Megan on the shoulder as their ice cream was brought. "You're not the first person I've had this talk with, and you won't be the last."

"He's not lying, lady," The waitress interjected. "Tall man's here all the time."

"Wait," Megan caught on. "She knows?"

"She does." Caine nodded. "Just overhearing conversations between others and myself. The thing is, she could go out and tell the whole world. Not a soul would believe her."

The waitress shrugged as she walked off.

"I don't understand." Megan confessed as she took a drink.

"Imagine you were her." Caine pointed to the waitress as she walked away. "Overhearing all sorts of things all the time. Then, someone like me comes in and starts talking crazy. Demons, angels, aliens, the whole nine yards. You go tell people, but you have no evidence. Is anyone going to believe you?"

"I would guess not," Megan concluded.

"You see," Caine continued the explanation. "People say there are conspiracy theories about everything. Many of those people are provable undiagnosed schizophrenics, gullible idiots, or they have no evidence. Their claims could be so outlandish that you would have to be insane to listen. So, no one with any power, or education, believes them. Since the educated don't believe them, why would the masses? It makes my job a lot easier to let you humans do that to yourselves. Think about it. You've been to Jon's class, right? Did anyone seem like they believed anything he was talking about."

"We haven't even had a lesson yet." Megan laughed.

"Seems like him." Caine smiled so wide his lipstick cracked. Megan could not help but chuckle a little to herself about how normal this was all starting to feel. "People pay for a full class and he gives half a one because he was out the late the other night."

"Caine?" Megan finally was starting to feel comfortable. "The way you just said, 'you humans.' You're not human either, are you?"

Caine shook his head confirming Megan's thoughts.

"What are you?" Megan asked quietly.

"That's very complicated and difficult to explain, so I won't." Caine dug into his ice cream; a bit of lipstick came off on his spoon. "Just think of me as a friend. Caine Grimm isn't even my name. Your tongue can't pronounce it, and your ears can't even comprehend the sound of it. I got this name from an angsty seventeen-year-old demon and her boyfriend."

"Your lipstick is coming off," Megan finally gave in. The look was bothering her too much. "Right over there."

"Sorry." Caine pulled a small tube of lipstick out of his pocket and reapplied it. "Better?"

"Kinda." Megan squinted trying to get a better idea how to help Caine. Caine let out a sigh and dug in his pocket for his phone. He turned on the selfie camera and used it as a mirror to adjust his lips. "There you go."

"How can you see with those shades on all the time?" Megan continued sucking on her shake.

"I see wavelengths that you humans can't," Caine explained. "Keeping them on blocks some of the wavelengths and helps me see better. Any other questions?"

"Yeah," Megan nodded. "How did you find me and how did you call off the police? Are you with the government?"

"No." Caine took another bite. "My kind has been watching over you for ages. We do have an understanding with the authorities though. You wouldn't believe how hard it used to be to get that access to everything we needed. Luckily, some aliens decided that drunk flying around Roswell was a good idea. As soon as we were able to explain it to the President himself, it opened all sorts of doors for us."

"Does that mean your with..." Megan's eye grew large.

"The men in black is a strange concept," Caine did nothing but adjust his tie and look proud of himself. "You all spread it amongst yourselves when your people started taking better photos and figuring out some things are more than legend."

"Holy shit." Megan's eyes grew large. "Holy fucking shit. That explains the badge you flashed my roommate."

"Humans are so easy to deceive." Caine pulled out the badge from earlier. Megan took it. "Show you all a shiny piece of metal and act like you have authority and you can get them to do whatever you want."

"This looks like it's from a toy set at a dollar store." Megan smiled at the absurdity and handed it back.

"You sound better." Caine pointed out.

"Honestly," Megan agreed despite herself. "As weird as all this shit is, talking to you kind of putting it all into perspective. What I saw may have been strange to me, but to you, Jon and Alegra, it is just another day. Speaking of, is she alright?"

"Everyone is fine," Caine reassured her that she was fine, and that everything was under control. "It takes more than a few punches and a knife to keep her down. I've seen her get shot and act like it's just a mild annoyance. She's probably getting her fill right now. Knowing that crew, Jon will probably help her butcher what is left. The two of them will clean the mess."

"What about the guy?" Megan asked. "The guy that attacked her. Won't someone come looking for him?"

"No," Caine shook his head. "That's where I'm going next. I'll go back and see if we can figure out who he is. After that, I can just make all records of him disappear. People will remember him, but according to government records, he will have never existed."

"I see." Megan never realized that it could be that easy for anyone to just be wiped from history. "You can make people just disappear like that?"

"Want any more?" Caine changed the subject and finished off his ice cream.

Megan shook her head.

"Tell you what," Caine felt he was getting a good understanding of Megan. "I think you have a good head on your shoulders and understand what is going on. I'm going to tell Jon you are going to take a few days to recover and to contact you after that. Is that ok? Or if you prefer, you can just walk away now. I'm sure he would understand."

"I can't," Megan tapped her fingers against the side of her glass. "Those guys came for Miko, and she needs help. They may not stop coming for her if something isn't done. Especially if that Maximillian Grool the mentioned, keeps ordering them too. I'm not going anywhere. I'm just not sure if I can face Alegra without thinking about what I saw, though."

"That makes sense," Caine stood up and tossed a single hundred-dollar bill on the table, and ushered Megan towards the door. "As I said, she feels horrible for what you saw. Take your time because she probably needs it too."

Chapter 11

Caine dropped Megan off back at her dorm room and taught her what to tell her roommate. He made sure to also give her his direct number in case anything else came up. She smiled and thanked him for putting everything into perspective before she closed the door.

The bar was still shuttered when Caine returned. Using an extra key Jon had given him years ago, Caine let himself in the back door; the smell of viscera and blood greeted his nostrils. From somewhere within, he could faintly make out the sound of flesh being cut. No, Caine shook his head at the thought. Cut was a bad way to describe it. It sounded more like it was being torn. When Caine entered the main bar room, he found Jon off to the side, preparing a pile of large freezer bags and plastic storage containers. Alegra was on all fours enjoying what was probably her first fresh meal in ages.

"After you left, she calmed down." Jon stood up and walked over to Caine. "Her hunger took over from there.

Normally, she would have just tore into the guy. I guess realizing she was protecting Megan helped her to keep herself under control for a little bit. Speaking of Megan, how is she?"

"Better." Caine rubbed his chin. "Megan just needed what she saw explained to her. Is Alegra still eating him? She usually doesn't keep eating so hungrily after they die. I wonder why she's still devouring him."

"He's not dead." Alegra sat up and swallowed a large bit, after using her hands to tear it into smaller chunks.

"What?" Caine moved in closer. Alegra instinctively growled at him as he moved in, but then apologized between bites. Caine looked closer at the man. When he moved in, the man's eyes instantly focused on Caine. He was currently missing a lower jaw, but it looked as if he was begging for help. Caine stood up and nodded.

"See?" Jon tried to confirm with Caine. "Our friend is still alive."

"Do we know who he is?" Caine turned to Jon.

"Alegra won't stop eating long enough for me to check for any ID," Jon sighed fed up with trying. "So, I got some containers for leftovers. Got to do something while I wait."

"You know there is another way." Caine was confused as to why Jon had not tried his other method. He rubbed his chin as he watched the grotesque scene before him.

"Thought about that," Jon nodded, "but you know me. I don't have the stomach to kill anyone."

"It would be mercy," Caine reminded him.

"Then you do it." Jon assigned the task.

Without another word, Caine walked back to the man and lifted one of his feet over the man's head. With a solid stomp, the top of the man's head was no more. Grey mess and blood began to spill out over the fake wooden floor. Jon reached behind the counter and pulled out a roll of paper towel and put it on the countertop. Caine took a seat and took his shoe off to begin cleaning it.

The body did not even have the strength to convulse, but it was obvious that the man's consciousness was shifting off its mortal coil, as his eyes began to lose focus. Jon moved quickly to the man's side. Alegra glared at Jon, disappointed, but did not make a sound as he put his hand on the cheek of the freshly made corpse.

Jon had wished it were always this easy when he had to communicate with the dead. He had explained to Alegra and Caine once before that the closer the spirit is to death, the easier it was to talk to them. He did not have to go through the whole calling to them, coxing them out with bait; none of it. A simple bit of contact, usually through touching the skin, and then just talking to their spirit was all it took.

"Wakey wakey," Jon looked at a blank space above the body. Nothing came.

"Jon," Alegra touched the necromancer's arm with a bloody hand to get his attention. "He's still not dead."

"What?" Jon looked confused.

"I noticed earlier," Alegra explained as she stuffed another piece in her mouth, "he tasted funny. I didn't think anything of it, but his heart just started beating again."

"What?" Jon questioned and looked at the body. The dead man's eyes began to focus again. Without a word, Alegra motioned for Jon to open his mouth. Jon did so and Alegra stuck a bloody finger in his mouth. Jon felt as she gently played with his tongue trying to hit all the different taste areas.

"I would prefer if you two keep the sexual cannibalism for when I'm not here," Caine mentioned.

103

"Jealous?" Alegra quipped as she went back to her meal. It had always amazed Jon and Caine how much she could eat when her meal was fresh. No bothered to answer her as she would not have heard it anyway.

"She's right," Jon confirmed. "It tastes funny. Like kissing someone who just finished a cigarette. It tastes like ash."

"Thrall?" Caine questioned as he squatted down close to the body, wiped a bit of blood off on his finger and licked it. "He's a thrall. Someone fed him vampire blood before sending him here. That might be why he's still alive. He's got vampire durability and the accelerated healing is keeping him alive."

"Sorry," Alegra interrupted. "I'm not too up on my vampire lore. I didn't even know there was any near here. What do you mean by thrall?"

"Just a minion," Caine explained. "They are usually told they are being made into vampires by drinking their master's blood. So, they do it. It gives the vampire slight control over the human. They can be useful when they need something done in the daylight. Just another way for them to control idiots."

"There are vampires in New Hancock?" Jon asked, looking for confirmation.

"One or two," Caine informed him, "but none that I know go by Grool."

"Maybe someone new moved into town," Jon suggested.

"If this guy would just die," Caine sighed "we could ask him. But since that isn't happening and someone already took his jaw off, that might be a little difficult."

"No, it isn't." Alegra chimed in as she stood up and moved to his head. She put her feet on his shoulders, and after putting her hands around the man's teeth, she gave a

104

hard pull. Slowly, the man's flesh began to tear. The muscle underneath gave way first and the separation was easy to see when the skin came next. Soon, what was left of the man's head was in her hands. Without a word, she handed the severed head to Jon and went back to munching. Alegra stood up when the chest stopped rising, and his heart stopped beating. She gave a disappointed *tsk* and left the body alone.

"I really wish she didn't do that like it was nothing." Jon mentioned as he set the head down on a table.

"Umm..." A quiet voice piped up from the corner. "Master Jon?"

Miko stood there, slightly shaking, but still trying to be brave.

"Miko!" Jon quickly rushed over to the nekomata. "I'm so sorry. We got so caught up in what..."

"She does eat people," Miko quietly confirmed to herself. "I wasn't seeing things the other night."

"Yes," Jon nodded his head, and moved to comfort her, "she does eat people, but she only eats bad people. People who want to hurt you again."

"I know..." Miko's eyes grew. "I knew him. He used to hit me. If I didn't please enough people. He would scream and beat me."

"You knew him?" Jon asked looking for Miko to affirm her identification. Miko nodded without a word.

"Why didn't you say this sooner?" Alegra added slightly ashamed as she turned to her.

It was obvious that something about Alegra changed. Her voice growled less. Her prey was, finally, truly dead, and there was no rush to eat.

"I thought he might have not recognized me." Miko looked down at the now lifeless body. "He didn't say anything when I tried to help them earlier. Also, you kept telling me that was my job to help people and collect tips."

"I'm sorry." Alegra wanted to approach Miko and comfort her. She thought better of it when she considered her current state. Instead, she leaned against the bar and crossed her arms. She searched the words to convey how she felt. "If I knew, I would have thrown them out."

Miko shook her head. Tears began to well up.

"You saved me from them again." Miko walked closer to the body then passed it and approached Alegra. With a smile on her face, she put her arms around the waist of the demon, not even minding the blood at all. "You saved me again."

Alegra did not know what to do, so she used her clean biceps to try and hug the nekomata back. After a minute, the cat woman broke away and looked back at the body on the ground before her; hissing slightly, she spit on him.

"He'll never hurt you again," Jon reminded her as he stood behind Miko. She gazed absently, lost in thought, at the spittle that pooled on the body. "I'm about to make sure of that right now."

Jon took the head off the table and put it close to the body. He then put his hand on the half of the cheek that remained.

"Wake up, you son of a bitch," Jon spoke in a commanding tone. A small gray figure began to materialize over the severed head. Jon glared as it slowly took the form of the man on the floor, albeit now naked.

The figure did not move.

"I don't want none of your shit," Jon scowled. "I'm going to ask you some questions, and you have two choices. One; you answer them, and then I take you within me. Two; you don't say shit, I send you to the afterlife and you burn in Hell for your crimes against this woman right here."

The figure was quiet. It motioned that it could not speak.

"You are too fresh," Jon pointed out, already exasperated by the behavior of the spirit. "I've been doing this for long enough. You are not fooling anyone, and you sure as Hell aren't fooling me. You can talk as easily as you used to beat her. You talk when I tell you to. Do you understand me?"

"Yes," The figure reluctantly spoke.

"I need your name," Jon crossed his arms and stared down at the ghost.

"My name was..." The ghost started.

"No," Jon shook his head. "I don't want any pretentious bullshit 'I was...' answers. You will be quick and concise. You have hurt people that are my friends and right now, I'm the only thing stopping you from being sodomized by a three-foot spiked demon dick. You think being eaten alive was bad? Wait until you see what is waiting for you if you don't cooperate with me. All you are is a little piss ant that needs to hurt those weaker than him to feel powerful. You hear that? A fucking piss ant, not even a fucking man. So again, you are to answer what I am asking, or you will burn for your sins. You are my bitch. So, you will fucking answer me."

The figure said nothing.

"Right." Jon walked off visibly pissed. "Calling my bluff."

Jon made a wave of his hand and soon a black portal began to form under the ghost. Black hands began to reach up and grab at his bare legs. A look of panic formed over the figure's face as it tried to free itself. It was in vain as a few arms finally got a hold of his leg and began to drag him into the hole.

"Ok," The ghost finally called out. "John McGee."

"Good." Jon made a wave again and the hole began to close. The now smaller hole allowed the spirit to grip each side and begin to pull itself free from the hole. "Where did you get the vamp blood?"

"What?" The ghost asked. Jon walked closer and with a wave, the portal grew wider and the man lost his grip with one hand, leaving him dangling dangerously above the widening hole. "I don't know what you're talking about. I swear. Before we went on any jobs, the boss would give us all funny tasting shots. Said it would help with our courage."

"Who's the boss?" Jon glared into the spirits blank eyes. The spirit was too preoccupied with escaping to answer.

"Is he a vampire?" Jon asked gently playing with the size of the hole.

"I don't know," The spirit panicked. "I have no idea what you're talking about."

"Who is the boss?" Jon asked.

"Grool," The man's eye begged for help. "He ran the club where I worked."

"Wrong." Jon shook his head.

"What?" The spirit panicked. "You met him."

With a wave of his hand, Jon widened the hole again. By doing it quicker, it caused more hands to reach up and grab the man at the shoulders. The greedy hands then ripped him into the hole with a scream that caused even Caine to shudder.

"Bruce Springsteen." Jon waved again and the portal closed.

"Is he gone?" Miko asked softly, breaking the silence that had followed Jon's actions.

""He's going to pay for what he did to you." Jon informed the cat girl. "Hell isn't going to be fun for him. Caine, you feel like going on a quick road trip?"

"Where?" Caine leaned back against the bar.

"He said that the drink came from Grool," Jon tried to breathe and calm down. He hated doing what he had just done. Jon had lost himself when he found out the man was not only part of keeping Miko captive but beating her as well. "Vampire blood might not hold power outside the body long. So, my guess is there is a lair close to the club. I want to go check it out."

"I doubt that would be a good idea," Caine interrupted Jon's train of thought. "They're probably expecting a retaliatory attack tonight. He may have brought in more security to make sure it's much more fortified."

"What do you suggest?" Jon's voice made it obvious he did not like not going tonight but knew Caine was right.

"I said earlier that there are a few vampires in New Hancock." Caine pulled out his phone and checked a few things. "They might know something. We can make an unexpected visit. They won't like it, but they'll get over it."

"You're going tonight?" Alegra interrupted.

"Yeah," Jon agreed to the plan as he used a few paper towels to clean off his hands. "If what Caine says is right, and there is an unknown vampire in town, the others aren't going to like that and may take this matter into their own hands. Could lead to a body count of thralls. That leads to hunters moving into the area, and an even higher innocent body count. They'll kill it if it isn't right in the eyes of God. I can't let that happen."

"You move fast," Alegra scolded Jon with concern. "You move stupid. You move stupid, and you get hurt."

"We don't have a choice," Caine agreed with Jon. "A war would bring hunters and that is way too much of a hassle for me."

"Who's going to help me with this?!" Alegra got visibly upset motioning to the bloody mess on the ground.

"I will..." A soft voice came from the side of the room. Miko sheepishly raised her hand. "You saved me twice. It's the least I can do."

With a groan, Alegra relented and nodded.

"Do you take showers well?" Alegra spoke to the cat. "Because I am not getting scratched up bathing you."

With a slight laugh, Caine exited out the door he came in. Jon attempted to do the same, but a hand grabbed his shirt.

"Don't be stupid, Jon." Alegra turned the man around to face her. "You don't do well with vampires."

"Aww..." Jon teasingly booped the demon's nose. "You're worried about me."

"No asshole," Alegra, annoyed, pushed the man's hand away. "Your name is on the lease to this place. I kind of need you alive."

Jon felt that small act of concern calming the earlier rage inside him.

"I'll stop by before I head home." Jon looked around trying to avoid her gaze. "Help you finish cleaning if you need it. Anything else happens, call us. We'll come scrambling back. Caine knows what's going on, and I'll follow his lead."

"Ok," Alegra relented. She trusted the two of them, but it still did not sit easy with her.

Jon walked out of the bar after Caine. Alegra sighed heavily and leaned against the bar. Her mind distracted by thoughts of whatever the two were going to do going horribly wrong.

"I used to have that same look for some of my favorite customers." Miko interrupted the silence that came after Jon left.

"Shut up, cat." Alegra responded flatly.

110

Chapter 12

"Alegra's worried about you." Caine threw out as the car sped down the highway. Jon stared out the window as he pressed a button and rolled the window down. He pulled a pack of cigarettes out of his pocket, slapped the top against his hand a few times and pulled one out. He lit the stick, inhaled and then exhaled the smoke.

"She just needs me to keep the business going." Jon checked his watch. The time was now pushing three in the morning.

Jon rolled down the window down further to make sure the smoke did not make its way back into the car. He flicked some ash out the window absentmindedly as the car sped further into the early morning.

"You're distracted," Caine pointed out. "You need to snap back to reality."

"Yeah," Jon agreed as he tossed the lighter, which he had been toying with, into the cup holder. "Just getting tired is all. It's been a long day."

"Sorry," Caine apologized, "but bring your mind back in the game. I don't want to have to explain your death to those two because you couldn't stop thinking about what just happened."

Jon silently took another drag.

"Anyway, why did you send him to the other side?" Caine questioned. "He could have been useful."

"I didn't," Jon explained taking another drag. "I forced him to come with me. The hands were others in me trying to escape. Too many hands trying to use him as leverage pulled him in. I'm not sure what it's like in my head, but I'm guessing it pretty much is Hell. It might make him more talkative later."

"Smart." Caine pulled the car up to a house on the outskirts of town. Cars were parked down the street and loud music came from inside. "This is the place."

"Loud, vampire party," Jon pondered as he flicked his dead cigarette out the window. "This time of night, it's a great way to get the cops called on you."

"Anyone with power is probably already here," Caine explained to the professor. He found a parking spot for the car. "They have to keep their influence over the town somehow."

"How do we do this?" Jon asked, climbing out of the car.

"Pretend like we belong," Caine informed him as he did the same. "Find the host and see what he knows. We cause too much of a ruckus and they'll be on us."

"Good thing you're here," Jon admitted as he put his hands in his pockets and followed Caine to the front door.

A lone guard stood outside the door. His arms were crossed, and he was already glaring at the two as they walked up the steps. As the two men approached, the guard reached for a sidearm but did not pull it out of the holster.

"Invitations," The guard barked as he stopped the two at the door.

"I don't need one," Caine responded as he stared down at the man.

"Yeah?" The guard scoffed. "Well, my boss does. If you don't have one, then fuck off."

"Hey," Jon interrupted as he began to slur his speech. "I really gots to pee. We saw a par...party and thought I could use the pisser. Jus' a lil bit."

Caine knew he should have stopped the improv Jon had thrown in but did not want to break the idea, or the guard's neck, to gain access. He had also guessed the man was a thrall to the vampire holding the party, and that money was not going to do the trick. So, seeing what Jon had up his sleeve might as well be next plan that go to.

"No," The guard stood firm.

"Can I use those bushes?" Jon asked, almost falling over on Caine until the tall man caught and straightened him.

"Sure." The guard figured it would not hurt. "You just aren't getting inside. Big guy here stays with me."

"You are a good man." Jon patted the man's strong shoulder and then gave him a thumbs up. Jon nodded to the scowl the man gave him, then staggered around the corner.

Caine stared down at the guard. Neither of them backing down.

"Your friend has been gone for a while," The guard broke the minute or two of silence.

"He's drank a lot," Caine replied never once taking his gaze off the guard.

A gray woman appeared from around the corner and seemed to float towards the two men. The woman looked no older than her early twenties and had a strange ethereal flow about her. Her long hair shimmered and flowed away into an abnormal fog. A long, white, skin-tight dress of fog flowed down and hugged every curve along her body. The guard was instantly mesmerized.

The figure put her hand on Caine and gently moved him out of the way. She then ran her hand along the guard's face and onto his chest. With a bit of a smile, she moved her hand down to his belt and slid the excess out of the loops. She used it as a handle to try and pull the man away from his post. At first, he was hesitant, but after what one could only call a carnal, irresistible smile from the spirit, the man gave in and followed.

As soon as the two were out of sight and around the opposite corner of the house, Caine let out a whistle. Jon appeared from his side of the house and rejoined Caine as the two stepped inside the building.

Jon was asked quite often why he did not have much knowledge of vampires. He explained he found them to be over studied and wanted to focus on lesser-known creatures. Within just a few minutes of being inside the party, he found the myth about them being very sexually driven to be true. The party had more bodies making out, with some even having full-blown intercourse, than a college party porno.

"Who was that?" Caine asked, scanning the rooms as he looked for the host. A rather provocatively dressed maid with a tray of wine offered one to both Caine and Jon.

"Hooker I found bleeding out a few years ago," Jon said as he accepted a drink and pulled out his wallet to put a dollar bill in the waitress's tray. The waitress declined and lifted her skirt showing the many dollars that had been slipped into her G-string. Jon, not wanting to be rude, was happy to oblige. Caine politely declined.

"I wouldn't drink that," Caine informed Jon as he took a sip of the wine.

"I was only pretending to be drunk," Jon said as he downed the rest of the drink. "Got to do something to calm the nerves. I don't do well with vampires."

"It's there to sweeten your blood," Caine explained the purpose to Jon as they moved to the upstairs portion of the house. Jon almost tripped over a couple on the stairs following him. "It's also to lower your inhibitions. To put it bluntly it's not for you..."

"It's for me," A deep male voice interrupted Caine's explanation.

"It's for him." Caine pointed to a man about Jon's height, wearing a luxurious black suit with a purple shirt. Three earrings adorned his right ear, and his long dreadlocked hair was tied loosely behind his head. Two armed guards flanked him.

"I don't recall inviting you, Grimm." The man glared at the two intruders.

"Dr. Jonathan Bringer," Caine began with introductions. "This is Malcolm deCont."

"Nice to meet you," Jon greeted the host as he reached his hand out with a smile.

"Shaking hands is too plebian for vampires," Caine corrected Jon's faux pas. "It's also a sign you don't trust them. To them it's a way for people to check each other for hidden blades."

"I'm sorry, Malcolm," Caine said, turning his attention to the presumed host of the party. "He's not well studied on vampire culture. Spends a lot of time with ghosts,"

115

"You're the necromancer," Malcolm stopped Jon's lesson from Caine by waving that conversation off. "I've heard of you. I was wondering when our paths would cross. That still does not explain the intrusion, however."

"We need information," Jon explained. The vampire finally let his annoyance at the new intruder show.

"You leave." Malcolm waved Jon away. The two guards quickly flanked Jon and began to escort him out.

"It's about a possible intrusion of New Hancock territory," Caine continued, not attempting to help Jon as he was led out of the house.

"Intrusion?" Malcolm motioned for Caine to follow him into what can only be described as a throne room. A large chair rested against a wall, and purple drapes covered the walls of the room. Lit torches added a flair of mystic lighting to the room.

"Bring Jon back and we'll talk." Caine stood in front of the throne as Malcolm took a seat and crossed his legs. With a snap, one of the guards used a walkie talkie to order Jon into the room. After a minute, Jon was led in.

"Grabbed a second drink." Jon held up new a champagne flute.

The vampire glowered at Jon, but he did not say anything.

"A friend of ours was attacked," Caine explained. "The blood tasted of ash. Sounds like a new vampire has entered the town. The name we have is Maximillian Grool. Ring any bells?"

"You tasted it?" Malcolm got a chuckle. "Something you mean to tell me about yourself, Grimm? Sounds like you might be interested in joining our ranks."

"Our friend bit him in the fight," Jon quickly explained. "She mentioned something about it so both of us tried it."

"How does your friend know how blood should taste?" Malcolm leaned in and folded his fingers in front of his chin.

"Ever bite your lip?" Jon threw out a quick explanation trying not to laugh slightly at the absurdity of the question. He knew Malcom was digging for more information than the two were willing to give. By batting it away so quickly and flippantly, Jon hoped to use the annoyance he had already built up to end the line of questioning quickly and have the attention turned to Caine.

"Fair point." Malcolm sat back and motioned for the guards to come closer. Jon felt a bit pleased at himself that his ploy had worked. "Tell everyone the party is over. I have a feeling that tonight is going to not allow me to continue the party mood."

"I don't trust them," One of the guards attempted to balk the order.

"You see that tall man?" Malcolm pointed at Caine. "If he wanted us dead, we would be. Now, end the party."

The guard sized up both Caine and Jon but left quietly.

"I didn't want them to hear this," Malcolm explained. "Frankly, I don't even want to tell you. However, I feel I owe it to both of you for telling me about this intruder. I think it is fair to say you are going to ask about thralls? That's what the ash taste you are referring to lead you to believe. When a mortal drinks vampire blood, it does nothing. No different than what happens when drinking another mortal's blood. It is a mind game played from centuries of superstition. Would you care to try?"

Malcolm held out his wrist. Caine shook his head.

Jon froze. Something in him wanted to try it. He said had never studied vampires, and this may be his closest shot.

On top of that, after the faux pas from earlier, a sign of trust might be a good thing.

Jon stepped up to the throne and froze again. Malcolm told him to just bite down. Caine made no motion to stop Jon as he bit into the vampire's wrist. Jon was amazed at how little pressure it took to open the wrist. Cold blood pumped into Jon's mouth. Malcolm was right, there was no ash taste.

"See?" Malcolm pressed his hand against his wrist for a second and the bleeding stopped. "How do you feel? Satisfied?"

Jon mentally searched his body for a few seconds and found no change.

"Slightly disappointed," Jon admitted. "I was hoping something would change; anything. There was nothing."

"Exactly," Malcolm nodded. "Modern times do call for modern solutions though. Usually, a drug in the blood is harmless to us but will addict humans. Get them addicted to that and it helps control them just a little more. I hope I have been able to help you, but I don't have anything left to say. You have, however, made my next few nights remarkably interesting."

"Thank you, Malcolm." Caine bowed slightly and motioned for Jon to do the same. "You've actually told us a lot. I hope the sun never rises on your face."

"May you enjoy it for the both of us." Malcolm returned the bow. Caine began to leave and motioned for Jon to do the same.

Jon and Caine left the room and the party. Caine started the car as Jon pulled out another cigarette and rolled down the window. He lit it and took a long drag. Caine pulled the car back on to the street as Jon let out the smoke.

"Why didn't you stop me?" Jon asked as Caine stopped at a stop sign. "From drinking his blood that is. You told me it would make me a thrall."

"Malcolm and I have a working agreement," Caine explained, "similar to ourselves. I pull a few strings here and there for him. He feeds me information when I need it. If I were to try and stop you, it would have made it seem like I didn't trust him. Then he would feel he couldn't trust me."

"So, you put me in danger," Jon interrupted his thought with a drag. "In order to save a relationship of yours?"

"Of course not." Caine gave an inhuman smile. "You put yourself there."

Jon could not think of a clever response, nor could he think of a good argument. He just finished off his cigarette and pulled out his phone. The symbol for a text message appeared on the screen with the name "Maria" next to it. Jon just turned the phone off and put it back into his pocket. He reached for another cigarette. He did not want to read it. It would only make this bad night worse.

.

Chapter 13

Megan laid back on her bed in her dorm room. A notebook was open to a blank page next to her. Occasionally, she would look away from her laptop screen and write something down. Name, race, and various stats were starting to come together to make a character sheet. She then made a small note to thank her brother back home for sending her a pirated copy of the book she needed to make the character.

"Never thought you were into that kind of stuff." Megan's roommate leaned over to see what she was so intently staring at on the computer.

"I'm not," Megan replied looking away for a second. "It's for a date tonight. Guy wanted me to go check out his role-playing group. I agreed and now I have to make a character."

"That sounds like the most boring role-playing that could happen on a date." Megan's roommate let out a small laugh as she walked away and sat down on a futon across from the beds. She pulled some chips out of the cubby hole above it.

"I've been on worse." Megan admitted as she shrugged and the two shared a slight laugh.

Megan looked over the sheet one more time to make sure she had everything. She would have had to read the book to get the rules down, but she had not had the time between her classes. However, she figured a bunch of nerds in a basement should have no problem helping her. She was probably the only girl they have been that close to in a while.

She checked her phone and realized it was almost time to leave. She then flipped the screen over to the messaging app and checked for anything new. The only thing she had received recently was a reminder from Andy about coming to play with them tonight. She was tempted to text Jon and make sure everything was alright. He had canceled the latest class and she had not seen him since the bar fight. As soon as she reminded herself about that sight, a slightly queasy feeling came over her. She closed the app and got up from the bed.

Megan made her way over to the dresser and pulled out some fresh clothes. She then went to the bathroom and she started the shower. After a quick shower, she toweled off and began getting dressed. While her normal going-out style was centered around going to dive bar psychobilly and punk shows, she felt that that outfit would not be appropriate to do this time. A more conservative look that made her look more feminine, and out of her element. That would be perfect.

"My makeup is too dark." Megan opened the door of the bathroom. "Can I borrow some of yours?"

"How are you going to borrow it?" The roommate asked. "You gonna return it afterward?"

"You know what I mean," Megan called back. Megan's roommate told her to use it.

Megan opened the medicine cabinet behind the mirror and pulled out the most "normal" looking makeup she could find. She took her time and made sure every dot and dab were perfect.

"Thanks." Megan left the bathroom room.

"Holy hell," The roommate looked Megan over. "Where did my roommate go?"

"Traded her for a nervous girl out of her element look," Megan replied. "It's like nerd kryptonite."

"Nailed it." The roommate gave her approval.

"Awesome," Megan thanked her. She was not sure if it was sarcastic or not. Either way, if it worked, she could not have cared less. "Now, I'm going to trap myself in a basement with a bunch of sexually frustrated virgins and B.O."

"I'll pray for you," The roommate called out as Megan left.

The bus ride was a lot quicker than Megan had wanted, but it put her right where she needed to be. She had earlier uploaded the rule book into her phone for quick reference and had her notebook on her as well. She had to remind herself that this was more about finding out information on the demon burning down places, than about playing a game.

She knocked on the door of the home where she was told to be. Within a few minutes, an older woman answered the door.

"You must be Megan," The woman pleasantly greeted. "The guys are downstairs in their 'dungeon.' I think they have some soda and chips down there if you are hungry."

"Thank you very much." Megan made her way inside and was led through the suburban middle-class home and to the basement stairway. After a short climb down the stairs,

Megan was face to face with four guys huddled around a table.

"Guys," Andrew started. The load of paperwork and notes around him also led Megan to guess that he oversaw the game. "This is Megan. She wanted to come join our game."

"Dude," one of the guys that Megan did not recognize, rolled his eyes. "You don't need to try and bring your dates to games. We are knee-deep in Laksmir Caverns and don't need to be teaching noobs."

"I've played before." Megan lied, then "dropped" her notebook. She bent over to pick it up, giving the group a good look down her shirt. She could easily feel every eye in the place on her breasts. She could not help herself grin at how they were playing right into her hands. This was going to be shooting fish in a barrel.

After a little harmless flirting with the group while asking for help. She had made a few mistakes, but she felt confident enough to play again. However, she was still empty-handed on information about the burned down stirp club.

Everyone began to file out one by one as they had a bus to catch, or a ride had come and picked them up. Eventually, it was just Megan and Andy left. The way he had been staring at her all night had made this moment the most endangered she had felt all night.

"Did you have fun?" Andy asked as he moved closer to her as the two had begun to clean up the mess.

"Yeah," Megan acknowledged with a smile. She could see Andy getting lost looking in her brown eyes. "It was a lot of fun."

"You seem pretty cool about being trapped down here with all of us," Andy let out a nervous chuckle. "The guys drove off the last female members we had."

"I get it." Megan waved it off, but she could see how they would. She had no idea how to answer what she had just heard. "A bunch of introverts in a basement together, playing fantasy games. Probably don't get out much, and you all don't date a lot. It happens."

"Yeah, I guess," Andy ashamedly admitted as he set down his garbage bag. He had to change the subject quick. He did not want her to think that their little group was a bunch of luckless losers. "You're in Dr. Bringer's class, right?"

"Yeah," Megan had never noticed Andy in there, but had to admit to herself she never paid attention to her fellow students. That is unless she found them attractive. "Why?"

"Want to see something cool?" Andy smiled big.

Megan wanted to reach for her bag where she carried her mace but realized it was across the room.

"Sorry," Megan shook her head and slightly panicked. "We just met, and I'm on my rag and and…"

"What?" Andy was confused. "No no nonono… It's up in my room. That…that did not make things better did it?"

"Not in the least," Megan laughed.

"Ok," Andy put his hand up defensively. "I promise you, it's not my penis. That's not very cool."

Megan got a chuckle out of this. Out of the group, Andy easily seemed the most mature. Lucky for her, this led her to feel a little more comfortable about the situation.

"Ok," Megan finally agreed. She had no idea where it would lead. If they were alone then he might open up more about the arson. "Why not?"

The two walked up the stairs, through the living room, and up another flight of stairs. Andy's mom yelled something about leaving the door open and the two ignored her. It was a typical bedroom; a computer on a desk pressed against a wall, a tidy bed in the corner, and a shelf. Though, instead of trophies for various activities, sat a collection of PVC figurines.

Megan drew closer to them. Each one depicted the same type of girl. Big tits, long legs, and a happy or sexual look on their face. Megan would have chalked this up to him being a lonely nerd until she noticed one other characteristic about them that they all shared. Every single one of them had cat ears and a tail.

"Oh cool," Megan exclaimed looking at them, "Nekomatas?"

"Huh?" Andy stepped beside her. "No, those are cat girls. Sorry, probably should have hid those before bringing a girl up here."

"Haha," Megan laughed. "it's cool. You like what you like, you know? I mean, my mom always used to say cats were just reincarnated strippers. All they want to do is get on your lap and stick their butt in your face for money or treats."

Andy got a slight chuckle.

"I guess you're right there," Andy had a nervous tinge to his voice. "But that's not what I wanted to show you."

Andy moved over to a large rectangular object in the corner, covered with a towel. He took the towel off to reveal a dog crate. Inside the crate was not a dog, however. A small bipedal, green, scaled creature paced back in forth. Its reptilian eyes stared at the two as it froze upon seeing them.

"Redrum!" The creature cried out upon focusing on Andy.

"I taught him to say that." Andy leaned down and opened the cage. The creature watched Megan closely as it made its way out of the cage. "I call him Shorty."

"What is he?" Megan looked closer at the creature as it decided it was in no danger and turned its attention to a toy that had been sitting in the corner.

"No idea," Andy admitted. "Want to hold him?"

"Absolutely." Megan reached out as Andy picked the creature up and handed him to Megan. She could not help but instantly fall in love with the cuteness of the almost human-looking lizard thing. Without thinking, she reached for her phone and took a quick selfie with it.

"Whoa!" Andy exclaimed, and quickly snatched the creature back. "No pictures! I'm trying to keep it a secret."

"I'm sorry," Megan apologized quickly. "I just kind of I... I don't know. I should be going."

Megan excused herself and quickly left. Andy called out to her, but she ignored the shout. She had made it down the street before she let herself slowdown from the jog, she found herself doing. She had forgotten her notebook at Andy's, but right now she did not care. She had her keys, her phone, and something she had to show Jon.

When Megan was certain Andy was not following her. She found her way to the bus stop. Her transportation arrived almost as soon as she stopped by the sign. She took a seat and watched out the window as the bus pulled away.

Something clicked in Megan's mind after she took a minute to calm down. She pulled out her phone and opened a search engine in the web browser app. With the jostling of the bus, she was able to type out "Nekomata vs Catgirl." As the results came pouring in, Megan's eyes widened.

Chapter 14

A pounding came on Jon's office door. He did not have class, but it was a quiet day to catch up on some paperwork. A pounding on his door usually meant a visit from a student not happy about how many classes Jon did not have. He stood up and tried to remember the usual spiel he would give them. However, it was Megan who stood in his doorway.

"We need to talk," Megan said as she made her way past Jon and took a seat. In her hands were two cups of coffee. Jon decided it was best not to protest.

"About what you saw the other night…" Jon started the conversation.

"No," Megan stopped Jon from telling her anymore. She had already heard it. On top of that, her stomach still turned every time she thought about it. Even being in Jon's office was making her slightly nauseous. "Caine already explained that to me. I get it. I feel bad about running out like that."

"Alegra feels bad that you saw it." Jon reassured her as he made sure the door was closed.

"That's not what I came to talk about though." Megan sat down. "I need to talk about Miko."

"I told you to drop that," Jon sighed as he took one of the cups of coffee.

"I know, I know but…" Megan began.

"No buts." Jon rubbed his forehead. "Look, your job is just to do research. That's it. There are things out there that are a lot more dangerous than Miko or Alegra. Those things will kill you in a heartbeat. I don't want you getting mixed up in that. Just… just stick to the research."

Megan looked straight into Jon's eyes. She showed no sign of fear or regard to what he just said. She recalled what Caine had told her about not being top of the food chain, and how it no longer fazed her. She took a deep breath and pulled out her phone. She flipped through the photos and pulled up the selfie she had taken the night before. She tossed the phone on the table and leaned back in her chair; a defiant look came across her face as she waited for him to pick up the phone.

"You can threaten me," Megan stood up, tired of being told what to be afraid of by Jon. "You can tell me to fuck off. Jon, I'm not going anywhere. Over this past week, I've seen a world I never knew existed. I've drank with a demon, I've seen ghosts, and had ice cream with what I can only describe as one of the men in black. I am still standing. I am right here, and like it or not, I'm not going anywhere. I think, deep down, you know that. You didn't hire me for your little bull shit papers. You hired me because you need help with these projects. So, you're stuck with me."

Jon did not respond. He picked up the phone and looked at the image on the screen. He looked over at Megan as he handed her back the phone. Silently, he got up and walked to the door. He opened it and looked back and forth making sure the hallway was empty. He closed the door and locked it. He returned to his seat and leaned back.

"You've got some balls, huh?" Jon chuckled softly.

"My ovaries are fucking chrome," Megan responded proud of herself.

The passion in the woman's voice had turned his thoughts; maybe she was right. Maybe that passion in her voice was a genuine urge to help, and not just a rush to see more crazy things.

"Alright," Jon relented. "Whatever. I get it. You're not going to just sit in your dorm and type on your computer and get me the information I want."

"Nope," Megan replied with a smirk as she turned the screen off on her phone and put it back in her backpack.

"Caine ask you to do this?" Jon pondered.

"Nope again." Megan shook her head. "Miko needs help. People are still coming after her, and I'm not going to just tell her 'sorry' and hide. I don't see you, Caine, or Alegra doing that."

"That's our job." Jon leaned back and put his hands over his face in frustration.

"Well," Megan stood up and put both of her hands on the edge of Jon's desk, "Sounds like that's my job too."

"You're stubborn as hell," Jon laughed and motioned for her to sit down, which Megan did. "You know that?"

"My dad tells me that all the time," Megan boasted. "Says he wished his son had my drive."

"I bet. What was that photo supposed to show me?" Jon asked. "That you can find supernatural things on your own?"

"I thought you might recognize what I saw," Megan explained, sitting back down, "and that yeah, I can find this stuff too. I'm not afraid of the things that go bump in the night. Now, I'll tell you more if you tell me more. If you let me in on this little secret between you three."

"Alright," Jon groaned as he threw his hands up in defeat. "We use the code word 'Angels' to describe ourselves. As you're starting to learn, there exist two worlds. The world you know and a supernatural world. They mesh a lot more than you would think. At the same time though, they are separate. Separate rules, laws, and customs. However, just like in our world, some prey on others that can't defend themselves. People who want to hurt them; exploit them. There are those that don't see their lives and want to use them as science projects. We do everything we can to help those who need us.

"Miko is just such a case. We heard a rumor of a nekomata being used as a slave down at a strip club. So, we sent Alegra in to scope the place out. Once we found her, Caine and I went in to bust her out. The place got burned down. A few corpses were left. Price of doing business, so to speak. Caine covers our tracks with the authorities, and we will do it again when the need comes back up. Should have been the end of it, but some people apparently don't want to cut their losses."

"Just can't get this case to close, huh?" Megan confirmed.

"We think we're close," Jon explained. "A rogue vampire was running the joint. So, we let another of the city's vampires know he's intruding on their territory. Hopefully, it won't come to a war, and those after Miko will leave town."

"You keep calling her a nekomata," Megan interjected and slightly changed the subject. "I don't think she is."

"What makes you say that?" Jon raised an eyebrow. Hearing that he was wrong was not something he was expecting from his new protégé.

"It has to do with where I found that little guy," Megan pointed at her phone. "The guy who was taking care of him had these figurines on the wall. All of them looked like Miko. I mean not exactly, but the proportions. The big tits, the car ears, the tail. He corrected me when I called them nekomata. Said they were just cat girls. I looked it up and found articles where they were called 'nekomimi.' Means cat ears or something like that. Some sort of anime fetish, I think."

"I don't think I've ever heard of that." Jon pondered. He pulled out his phone and started looking into the term nekomimi on his own. He clicked an encyclopedia article for the word and sure enough, every image of them looked more like Miko than the images of the nckomata.

"See what I mean?" Megan added as he continued to scroll. "I mean there is some overlap, but only in modern video games and things like that. Like the game, makers are taking the lore and making it fit their world, not the legends."

"Send me that picture from earlier," Jon instructed Megan. She quickly pulled out her phone and sent the picture to Jon. Jon opened an image search and searched for the picture Megan had sent him. No results came up.

"Nothing," Jon mused as he shook his head.

Megan shrugged at the fact that nothing came up. She had no idea where to go from here and hoped that Jon would be able to help her. She hoped that he might know what the creature was and maybe know something about where it came from.

"What does that mean?" Megan asked, wondering if she had found a new creature.

"I don't know," Jon shook his head. "However, I have some contacts in The Library that might know something I don't."

"The Library?" Megan asked.

"The Library is a collection of mages and magic users," Jon explained. "They come together to share their studies on the supernatural world. Try and make sense of it for the betterment of humankind."

"You must be popular there," Megan mentioned, sipping her drink.

"I was expelled," Jon informed her without even a hint of shame. It was almost as if he was boasting his pride of that fact. "One of the most important things about being a member of The Library is the same as any place in academia: publish or perish. I refused to publish what I was assigned."

"What did they want?" Megan asked curious about Jon's past.

"Information on my wife," Jon explained and started to look uncomfortable. "I refused to give it to them."

"I didn't know you were married," Megan missed the social cue and continued her line of questioning.

"We're estranged," Jon shrugged hoping it would end the line of questioning. "I haven't seen or spoken to her in years."

"I'm sorry," Megan apologized, quickly realizing she was making Jon uncomfortable.

"It's not so bad." Jon waved the thought away and smiled. "If I ever want to be bossed around and bitched at, I'm sure Alegra would do it for a fee. Anyway, why don't you take off? I'm going to call an old acquaintance from The Library for drinks. Maybe he can explain a few things. You should come by the bar. I'll introduce you."

Megan thought about accepting the offer, but her stomach began to turn. All she could see was Alegra hunched over that man. Her teeth and hands ripping holes in him. The smell of his bodily fluids escaping and the look in his eyes as he silently begged her for help. His eye begging her to not let his life end like that.

"I don't think I can," Megan shook her head. "Not yet anyway. Sorry."

"I understand." Jon stood up and walked to the door. He unlocked it and held it open for Megan. "Take your time and lay low for a while. Try not to do any more undercover stuff unless I need you too. Please? Normally, if something bad happens, Alegra is the only one to give me a hard time. I think everyone over there has taken a shine to you, so I'd have to deal with all of them."

Megan nodded with a slight smile and agreed. She knew what Jon was getting at, but he understood she still needed some time to get the images out of her head. She headed out the door and checked her phone to find the time and headed to her next class.

Chapter 15

Jon checked his phone for about the millionth time since he had sat down at the bar at Misshapen. He had contacted one of his friends that remained in The Library and had set up a meeting. However, the contact's tardiness only caused Jon a sense of anxiety whenever he was needed. Getting caught contacting Jon might lead to worse consequences than expulsion. That was a thought Jon did not want on his mind.

"You know, checking your phone every two minutes isn't going to make Steve arrive any faster, right?" Alegra put another beer in front of Jon.

"I just wish he wasn't late everywhere he went," Jon took a sip and set the beer down. "I mean, the guy can open portals and can poof himself pretty much wherever he wants."

"I misplaced my keys," A male voice popped up behind Jon, "in Taiwan."

The owner of the voice gently clapped Jon on the shoulder which gave the necromancer a jump. The older man with short cut white hair and a well-trimmed bread, smiled as Jon turned and stood up to shake his hand. Jon motioned for him to take a seat, but the man walked behind the bar instead.

"Alegra," The man greeted the horned bartender. Alegra dried her hands of a towel from her back pocket. The man then gave her a hug, and kiss on the cheek. "You look as beautiful as always."

"Thanks, Steve," Alegra was careful not to accidentally hit the man with her horns. "What can I get you?"

"Just came back from vacation." The man walked back around and took a seat next to Jon. "So, whatever you have for a hangover."

"Jack and Coke," Alegra suggested and began pouring. "Hair of the dog that bit ya."

"So, Jon," Steve looked over at his old friend. "How's things? Teaching keeping you busy?"

"Hired a research assistant." Jon took a drink. "I would say so. The field research is making my ass drag though. Hard to keep up both."

"You can always try to come back to The Library," Steve suggested as Alegra gave him his drink. He thanked the bartender, pulled out his credit card, and a twenty-dollar bill as a tip. He tossed them on the table and the woman took it and put it in a glass next to the register. "We could help you out. Hell, you're probably doing so much double work."

"Why do that?" Jon laughed "When I can just pay for your drinks and you tell me what I need?"

"That way I don't get expelled for helping you." The man motioned for Jon to put his card back in his wallet after Jon pulled it out.

"I always thought danger was half the fun." Jon joked.

"Depends on what the fun is." Steve took a drink.

"I have some suggestions," Alegra gave her two cents.

"You're too expensive." Steve winked at the woman.

Jon pulled out his phone and found the picture Megan took and slid the phone over to Steve. Steve picked it up and looked at the picture. He scratched his beard and zoomed in the picture.

"She's cute," Steve laughed and set the phone back down. "Isn't she a little young for you?"

"Funny," Jon made sure the phone stayed with the older gentleman. "The creature she's holding. Does it look familiar to you? I can't say I've seen anything like it, or even read about anything like it."

"It doesn't look familiar," Steve shook his head and handed the phone back to Jon. "Looks like something out of one of those video games the kids are playing."

"You are not old enough to be talking like that." Alegra refilled Jon's beer. "You're what? Only a few years older than me maybe?"

"If only we could all be demons and look like we're still in our twenties," Steve took a big sip from the straw in his drink, "but my point still stands. I have never seen anything like that."

"If I sent this to you," Jon began to ask another favor of his friend, "do you think you could see what The Library has on it.

The old man scratched his beard again. He had given it a thought when Jon showed him at first but was waiting for his old friend to ask him. Again, Steve reminded himself that helping a non-member was punishable by expulsion from The Library. To help an exile, though, was something he didn't even know the punishment for. Nor did he want to find out. Usually, Jon would want minor things. How to aid an injured creature was the most common.

"I can't, Jon," Steve refused the request. He felt bad about it, but he did have to stick within the rules presented to him. Helping to heal was a whole different story. He could easily say he was researching aid methods for those creatures he helped. That would allow him to get away with what he did. This, however, was straight-up stealing information from The Library.

"I understand," Jon gave up asking further. He would continue to push but knew it would be futile. He rubbed the stubble that had started to grow on his chin while he thought.

"Alegra," Jon caught the bartender's attention. "Where's Miko?"

"She hasn't been feeling well," Alegra shrugged. "So, she's upstairs. She's been sleeping next to me lately. You might find her there."

"What do you mean?" Jon let concern slip through his voice. He had not been going through all this trouble to help Miko restart her life for her to just get sick and die on him. "Why didn't you call and tell me? I would have come over sooner."

"Figured she might have got in the garbage or something," Alegra explained. "I don't know how cats work."

"She's not a cat," Jon corrected Alegra.

"What are you two talking about?" Steve butted into the conversation.

"Can I take Steve up and introduce them?" Jon asked.

Alegra stopped and stared at Jon for a second.

"What?" Jon asked confused by her response.

"Can I talk to you in the back?" Alegra tilted her head towards where her office was.

Jon let out a sigh, and he followed her back there. Alegra closed the door behind him. What sounded like a hushed and muffled argument could be heard from behind the door. In the end, only Jon came out. He grabbed the set of Alegra's keys from next to the register, and he motioned for Steve to follow him.

The two walked through a door that led to Alegra's office and up a set of stairs to the front of her apartment. Jon unlocked the door, and the two took their shoes off in the kitchen. Jon and Steve made their way into the living room.

"Everything alright?" Steve asked.

"It will be," Jon answered looking around the room. "She'll be pissed and get over it. Not a big deal."

"I guess she is more woman than demon," Steve chuckled. Jon did not share in the joke.

"Miko," Jon called out. A soft groan came from the bedroom. True to Alegra's words, the woman laid above the blankets on the bed. Jon sat down next to her and her eyes appeared to come to life.

"Master Jon," Miko smiled weakly. Whatever movements she was making seemed stiff and difficult. Her skin was clammy and pale. "Sorry, I couldn't' work today. I'm so tired. Mrow."

"That's alright." Jon reached down to touch the woman's forehead. As soon as he did, that spot came to life with color, slowly. "Steve, this is Miko, she's a nekomata. We found her along the side of the road. She was like this a few times but seemed to spring out of it. We're trying to figure out where she came from and how to help her get back home."

Jon admitted to himself that he did not know what they were planning on doing with Miko. He also concluded that that was something they probably should have thought about before rescuing her. He figured "getting her home" was as good of a story to Steve as any other.

"Are those ears real?" Steve looked down at the creature.

"She also has a tail," Jon pointed out to the older gentlemen. A tail poked out through a hole in the pajama shorts she wore. Alegra must have modified a pair for her to make her appendage more comfortable. The tail went down and was tucked snuggly behind her legs. "See?"

"Can I touch her?" Steve asked, fascinated by the woman before him.

"Don't ask me." Jon motioned towards the woman lying on the bed.

"Miko, right?" Steve moved in closer. "My name is Steve. I'm a friend of Jon's, can I touch your ears? I've never seen anything like you before."

Weakly, yet less stiff than before, Miko nodded. The old mage gently touched her ears, but they shot back, a sign of uncomfortableness from the woman. Steve understood this and stopped.

"He's a mage," Jon explained to Miko. "Just like me. He's from The Library. They keep all kinds of information on people like you. He just wants to examine you. See if we can help you feel better."

Miko nodded in understanding.

Steve touched the side of her face to check for human ears and like Jon, found none. Also, like Jon, wherever he touched her skin, tended to spring to life.

"Miko," Steve leaned closer, "I want to try something. Can you roll over on your stomach? I want to try something. I'm going to use my hand to touch you from the top of your spine to your toes. It's just going to feel like I'm giving you a massage."

"I've given those," Miko meekly smiled. "But I don't have that hard, front tail to rub after to give you milk. Is…is that ok?"

Steve raised an accusatory eyebrow at Jon.

"I'll explain later," Jon quickly shot in.

"You'd better." Steve glared at his friend. Soon, the man had begun to rub his hands up and down the woman's spine. He moved them over the t-shirt she had on and moved them down, and over her hips and to her toes. After a second, he did the same thing in reverse. Even though the experiment was short, it wasn't before long that the color was back in Miko's body. She let out a big yawn and got on her hands and knees. She stretched out her arms by leaving them in position and leaning back as far as she could, wiggling her butt in the air. Then she arched her back down to stretch her legs and back. After another big yawn, she sat right up.

"I feel better, nyan!" Miko exclaimed much brighter than before. Her complexion and mannerism looked as if there was nothing ever wrong with her. She quickly threw her arms around the older man. "Thank you, Master Steve!"

"No problem, Miko." Steve smiled and patted the cat girl's head. "Glad you feel better. Now, why don't you continue to rest up here? Alegra has everything under control downstairs. Jon, let's go back down. Like you said, you have some explaining to do."

"Absolutely," Jon patted Miko's head and followed Steve out of the room. The two said nothing as they walked back down the stairs. The two remained silent until they were seated at the fresh drinks prepared for them.

"How is she?" Alegra asked as they sat down.

"She's better." Steve took a big drink. "Much better. Where did you find her, Jon?"

"We were driving down 73, you know where that strip club burned down?" Jon started. "We had heard a demon did it, one that didn't match Alegra's description, and wanted to check it out. Found her stumbling along the side of the road. So, we took her in."

"She gets like that a lot?" Steve asked. "Any reason why she's talking about giving hand-jobs?"

"I asked around," Alegra jumped in, "and that club wasn't really on the up and up. It was basically a brothel and you were getting a preview before you got to pay for the merchandise."

"I see." Steve rubbed his chin. The other two could clearly see the gears turning in his head. "Does she do that a lot? Get sick like that?"

"Occasionally she gets a little pale," Alegra explained, "but she perks up whenever Jon is around."

"How long have you had her?" Steve was completely ignoring Jon at this point.

"About a week or so?" Alegra answered. She was not too sure how long it had been.

"Ever seen her eat?" Steve nodded starting to put things together. Jon listened very intently.

"Nope," Alegra shook her head, "Tried to feed her... people food? Ham, tuna. She wouldn't take any of it."

"Of course," Steve had come up with a conclusion from his line of questioning.

"So, what was wrong with her?" Jon asked.

"She wasn't being fed," Steve concluded.

"She wasn't eating," Alegra protested.

"She's not what you all think she is." Steve downed the rest of his drink. He pulled out his phone and opened a search engine in the browser. He typed in nekomata and pulled up a bunch of pictures that look liked cats walking on their hind legs. "I've seen nekomata pictures. She looks nothing like that."

"You're right," Jon agreed.

144

"I've seen things that look like her in my trips to Japan. The Akihabara district of Tokyo to be exact." The old man typed in cat girls and pulled up pictures that looked similar to Miko. "She looks like a cat girl from their cartoon and comics. However, a few things are different. The eyes, her nose."

"She's literally a cat girl." Jon was slightly disappointed that he was wrong, and that Steve now confirmed it.

"Exactly," Steve nodded. "Now here's the kicker. Cat girls don't exist. Their just some dream thought up by some artist. Going on that, and what I saw when Jon touched her, I figured out what was wrong with her. She doesn't exist. She's probably some pervert's personal familiar."

"What?" Alegra was confused.

"Someone made her," Steve tapped his phone to close the screen. "I'm going to check with The Library and see if I can find the owner. Jon, you stole someone's familiar, and you don't even know how to take care of her. If you weren't already in hot shit you are now."

"Wait," Jon held up his hands as if to deflect the accusation. "You can see she was used for sex work. She doesn't even realize it was wrong what she was doing. You want to send her back to that?"

"Jon," Steve sighed deep, "it's not up to me. Rules are rules. You don't know what you could have. What knowledge someone is looking to get back from her."

"Let me solve this." Jon stood up next to his friend. "Here's the thing. You go and tell The Library an exile stole a familiar, and you know what they're going to say? Why were you with him? The fact that you didn't knock my lights out and take her right now, you just became an accomplice. You're in as deep as I am."

Steve did not say a word.

"Why do you always do this to me, Jon?" Steve groaned as he rubbed his eyes.

"Why do you keep helping me?" Jon smiled at the older gentleman.

"Cause she's too pretty to cry if you fuck up." Steve jabbed a thumb at Alegra. "I can't bear that thought. Also, for future reference, Miko, I think you called her, doesn't eat like we do. She feeds off magical energy. That's why when you and I touched her, she started to come back."

"Thanks," Jon patted his confidant on the back. The man just shook his head, and with a wave of his hand, he opened a portal behind him. He waved defeatedly at the two as he turned around and stepped through it. The portal closed silently behind him.

Alegra rolled her eyes and began ringing up the man's tab. After a few minutes, the portal opened back up and Steve stepped back through. He scribbled a bit on a receipt Alegra placed in front of him and took his credit card back. He reopened the portal and walked back through.

"Told you that was a bad idea." Alegra took a deep breath as she poured Jon a drink. "What are you going to do now?"

"I'm going to let Miko rest," Jon took a drink of the beer. He stared blankly at the wall. He knew Alegra was right. Contacting anyone in The Library was a bad idea, but he wasn't going to admit that. He was all out of ideas. So, the bad ideas would have to do. He decided there was only one place he had not checked as thoroughly as he should have. "I'm going to go out to a strip club."

"Not without me," Alegra tossed her dish rag on the table and left from behind the bar. "I'm not letting you go back out there alone."

"Stay here," Jon stood up and put his hands on her shoulders to stop her. There was not enough alcohol in his system to impair him, but there was enough to make him braver than he was. "Take care of Miko. People are after her and she's helpless alone. I'll just sneak in, see if I can find any sort of lair this guy may have had around there. Then I'll get out. I'll text you when I get home, and let you know I'm safe."

"And if I don't hear from you?" Alegra asked. The horned woman did little to hide the concern in her eyes. This was the second time in a week Jon had gone out and done something like this.

"Call Caine." Jon did not turn around as he gave the instruction on his way out the door.

Chapter 16

Jon flicked his second cigarette of the trip out the window. He checked how many he had left and was disappointed that there was only one. He cursed softly and could already hear voices in his head telling him that quitting would be a lot better option for him. Since he was not sure if that was his own subconscious or one of the many spirits that also inhabited his body, he decided to ignore it.

He was smart enough not to park the car in the club's parking lot but found a carpool lot that, according to his GPS, put him about a quarter of a mile down the road from it. He turned the directions off on his phone and stuffed the device in his pocket. He climbed out of the car and gently shut the door. He made sure not to lock it as he did. A quick escape might be needed if things went wrong.

The night air was still. Any sound would be heard for quite a distance. Bugs and even an owl could be heard in coming from the trees close to the side of the road. A few fireflies danced out in the distance. On any other night, this would have been peaceful. However, breaking into a vampire's lair was not a peaceful situation. Jon cursed his addiction as he felt another craving coming on due to the stress. If there were any guards around, the cigarette smell would be alert them immediately. He had to shelve the idea for now.

Jon found a clearing away from the view of the road and with a wave of his hand, brought out a gray figure to stand before him. It was the man that attacked Alegra in the bar. The spirit was too strong and too willing to need any magic words. Even for a spirit, the man appeared out of breath and gasping. Jon stared at him eye to eye.

"Welcome back." Jon gave the spirit a cocky grin.

"Where am I?" The spirit asked.

"Back in the land of the living," Jon informed him. "How was Hell?"

"The others told me I wasn't in Hell." The spirit was agitated. He tried to seem imposing, but Jon did not back down.

"Good for you," Jon gave the spirit a sarcastic thumbs up. The ghost was clearly not as amused as Jon was. "You figured it out. Let me bring you up to speed. You are my captive. I figured you would be useful, so I didn't let you cross over. However, I'm going to give you a choice. Continue to be useful to me, and you can stay with me. Piss me off at this point and I will let you cross over. You know what happens if I do that?"

"Three-foot, spiked, demon dick," The spirit replied.

"Three-foot, spiked, demon dick," Jon repeated confirming what the spirit thought. "And they say you thugs are just meatheads. Here is what you are going to do. You are going to accompany me to your old hideout. The strip club that we took that helpless cat girl from. You do as I say,

150

and you can stay with me. You screw up, demon dick. Got it?"

"Yes," The ghost sounded defeated.

"We're going to walk down there." Jon was amused at the spirit relenting so easily. "This should all look extremely familiar to you, right? When we get about a tenth of a mile from the place, I want you to go and scout it out. I want to know how many guards. I want to know their locations. You can easily come back into me and I'll see what you saw. Other than that, I am going to go look around the place. You tell me if someone's coming. Sounds easy, right?"

The spirit did not respond.

"Good." Jon began his trek down the road.

Jon began to see the club as he got closer. The spirit hurried ahead. At this point, Jon stopped and found a good hiding place. After a few moments, the spirit returned and floated into Jon just as he was instructed. As Jon repressed the urge to vomit and gag, his vision was soon clouded with what the spirit had seen. A few guards sat in front of the building. They had pulled a table from the inside and were playing cards. A box cooler of drinks sat next to them. A few empty bottles were scattered around.

The vision floated around to the back of the building to show the back entrance of the club. A lone guard stood there, enjoying a cigarette and the night air. The guard would occasionally check his phone before looking back out into the night sky.

"Hmm..." Jon thought for a moment. He needed to come up with a plan to get inside. Jon took his time and moved closer to the building so he could see things with his own eyes. The two guards in the front continued to play cards and drink. The guard at the back door just stared out into nothing. After going through a few plans, Jon finally figured the simplest plan would be the easiest.

Jon quietly picked up a small rock and crept up behind the two playing cards on the front porch. Both men were too focused on the cards on the broken wooden table to notice him as he quickly ducked to the side of the building. A dark shadow hid him quite well. He peered around the corner and made sure he hadn't been seen. With a deep breath, Jon threw the rock. The rock released a wooden smack as it hit the center post holding up the table with enough force to wiggle the table and make one of the beers fall and spill all over their game.

"What the hell?" One of the guards shot up as beer poured over his lap. "Your dumbass hit the table!"

"I didn't touch the damn table." The other guard defended himself.

"Like hell!" The first guard yelled back. His face was growing red with anger. Jon ducked back into the shadow and within moments he heard the sound he wanted. The two men began to fight. The sound of footsteps came soon after and Jon could feel his heart stop as they passed him without stopping. The third guard had come to see what the commotion was. Jon used the confusion to slip by and get to the back door.

Luckily for Jon, the building had been burned out enough that it looked that the door was only being held shut by a small hook latch on the inside. He pulled his driver's license out of his wallet and by placing it between the door and the jamb, Jon was able to unlock the door. Once inside, he quickly and quietly shut and relocked the door.

The fire had spread a lot further than Jon had guessed. He found himself in the kitchen with piles of uncleaned dishes and the stench of an unpowered cooler. Jon looked around and saw that most of the aluminum equipment was black and sooty. A few pieces here and there had melted in the head.

Jon left the kitchen, and this took him to the main room of the club. The fire had spread and devastated this area of the club. Jon was careful with his footsteps to make sure not to alert any guards that may be inside. The simplest snap of a breaking board could ruin the whole thing.

The vision from the spirit had not shown him the inside, but he figured that since the outside was guarded, there was no point in guarding the inside. Why guard where no one could get in? Jon considered sending the spirit back out to make sure but figured there was no real safe place for him to wait for it to return.

Jon made his way to the doorway the man had led him through when he first came to the club. Holes had been burned in the cheap walls of the hallway. Ash and broken doors littered the floor. Jon checked each of the rooms to see if the fire had opened a secret passage that would not have been seen otherwise. He finally hit pay dirt when he walked into a room with a large desk. This had to be the main office Alegra had told him about.

A large metal door that looked new was now exposed on the wall. When Jon moved closer, he found that it was a keypad lock. Jon tried a few combinations but got nothing. He smiled as an idea entered his head. He looked all around and found the manufacturer's name. He then pulled out his phone and found their website. After a bit more digging on the page, Jon found the exact name of the door and found the operator's manual. After a quick download to his phone, Jon searched the file and found that the default code was the same on all the doors. Jon figured it was as good as any other number and pushed it in. To his amusement, the door opened.

The room was pitch black. Jon pulled out his phone and switched on the flashlight and began searching what he guessed was the vampire's lair. He felt his heart rate rise with every inch he uncovered. He almost let out a yelp when he saw a coffin laying in the corner by a desk, and on the desk were a few candles. Jon picked them up and noticed they were electric. After finding the switch, Jon turned them on, and fake candlelight filled the room. Jon could tell now that the coffin lid was off and empty.

Realizing there would be nothing interesting in the coffin, Jon made his way to the desk. A leather cap sat on the desk. Jon picked it up and looked inside the hat. Long strands of hair sat inside the hat where they were trapped in the inner brim. Also, on the desk sat an envelope made of parchment paper designed to look fancy. From the feel of it, Jon could tell it was probably from the local office supply store. Something that nice had to be important Jon figured and stuck the letter in his pocket.

After going through the drawers, Jon found a few binders. He started flipping through the pages. The first was a log of patrons just using the club, the amount spent, amount the club made that day. The next one was a ledger of amounts made by each of the girls in the back rooms. Jon found an entry for "cat". He shuddered as he looked at the number of clients she served on a regular day. The final was expenses. Jon knew what he was looking for this time and tried to find any entry for "cat." Sure enough, he found the entry. He noted an amount with the words "Cash to kid. Keep number for more freaks." Noted in the margin. Jon turned the flash on his phone's camera and took a quick picture. The final thing in one of the drawers was a little black book. Jon opened it up and found it was a list of contacts. His search was interrupted when he heard the metal door behind him shut. Jon jumped slightly and dropped the book.

"Who the hell are you?" A familiar voice filled Jon's ears. Jon turned to be faced with what looked like the man who initially led him to the back when he first came to the club.

"You're Max Grool," Jon put a few things together and was able to introduce the man himself.

"And you're not supposed to be here," Grool gave a toothy scowl. Jon made sure to check for fangs but strangely did not find any. "I'm going to have to snack on those guards. Teach them to pay attention."

"Snack on them?" Jon stood up and grabbed the hat. He tried to position himself to make a run for the door.

"Of course." Grool did not move but intently watched Jon's every move as he tried to position himself to get out of the room. "A few friends of mine told me you were with that dominatrix bitch. Lucky for me, after she made a snack out of me, my boss made me into a vampire. Got all these kickass vampire powers."

"Your boss?" Jon questioned. He tucked the hat under his arm. He mentally cursed himself for dropping the black book when the door shutting startled him. He could not take his time a retrieve it now. "And who would that be?"

"Does it really matter?" Grool held an arm out emphasizing the question. Jon knew the question was pointless, but he had hoped that, like the movies, the bad guy was going to divulge his secret feeling already victorious.

"You're planning on killing me," Jon relented the point. "I guess not."

"You're smart." Grool started to move towards Jon. "Not smart enough to not leave well enough alone."

"Didn't have a choice when your goons attacked my friends," Jon pointed out as he moved closer to the door. His confidence was waning, but curiosity told him that standing his ground was a better option. Maybe it was time for him to see a little bit of these "kick-ass vampire powers" for himself.

Jon motioned with his hand to summon the ghost from earlier to run interference. However, it was stopped when Grool lunged at Jon. A hand quickly caught Jon around the throat and began to squeeze. Jon could feel his eye begin to bulge slightly as his veins were being closed off from the pressure. Then, trying to use his "vampire strength," Grool tried to lift Jon but failed. Jon then landed a swift kick straight to Grool's groin. To Jon's surprise, Grool reacted. His eye grew wide and he released his grip. Jon used this moment to throw a punch at Grool's head. The man had collected himself enough to dodge the punch and tackled Jon to the ground with a hard slam, knocking the wind out of him. Jon struggled to catch his breath, but the vampire was soon on top of him.

Grool pushed Jon's head to the side, exposing his neck. This was the moment Jon needed. In all his years of doing this sort of work, Jon had learned one thing during these scuffles. Fight dirty. Your opponent is trying to kill you. No need for honor.

Jon put his hand on the side of the attacker's face and then slipped a thumb right in the man's eye. He kept pushing until it was deep in the socket and a clear jelly was working its way around Jon's thumb.

Grool let out a howl and clutched at the remnants of his eye. Jon kicked Grool off him and ran to the door. He stopped, turned back, and grabbed the hat he had dropped in the scuffle. He gave the vampire a quick kick to the ribs and bolted out the door.

Running as fast as his legs could carry him, Jon busted his way out the front door, past the two guards that were still grappling on the ground. He never knew how fast he could run a quarter mile, but with as fast as he made it back to his car, Jon was thankful for the hours he had spent in the gym on the treadmill.

Jon fought with the keys to the car door as he heard the footsteps of the guards coming up behind him. Out of frustration he tried the handle, and when it opened, he remembered he had left the car unlocked. He climbed in, started the car, and jammed the gear shift into reverse. Gunshots rang out behind him, with one shattering his back window. Jon slammed the gear into drive and put the car over the grass, and onto the road and into the night.

Jon began to feel something stinging as he sped the car down the highway and the adrenaline began to wear off. He pulled off the side of the road and looked down to see a bloodstain begin to form near a hole in his shirt. He swore slightly and realized he probably was not going to make it home. Lucky for him, there was somewhere that was a little closer.

Alegra woke up to a pounding on her door. Miko yawned and stretched in her spot at the foot of Alegra's bed. Groggily rubbed the sleep from her eyes, Alegra got up and put on a pair of pajama pants. She opened the door and Jon nearly collapsed in her arms. Cursing at the man in concern, she helped the semi-conscious Jon to her shower.

"Miko!" Alegra called out. "Miko get some towels. Jon, I need you to stay with me. What happened?"

Jon could not respond. Blood covered the front of his shirt and dripped into the tub. She figured she would ask him in the morning. Right now, it was time to get him fixed up.

Chapter 17

Jon rubbed his eyes and tried to ease the pain of the morning sun from his sore and tired senses. He was on his couch. He did not remember how he had gotten there, but he knew that home was not the place he drove to last night. Or was it this morning? Frankly, Jon did not care. He was alive and that was all that mattered.

The tiny apartment only had room for a couch and TV. There were very few windows. Due to this, when Jon moved in, he had painted all the walls sky blue. At least that way he would be able to see some form of a "sky" on his late nights. A door to the bathroom was around the corner and behind him. Across from that was a door that led to his study and bedroom. Jon had always laughed to himself that he should have given Alegra this apartment when he bought the bar and took her larger living quarters.

Jon looked down at the dirty coffee table in front of him. His smokes laid there. He reached down and grabbed the pack. When he did, he felt something other than cellophane on the package. A small sticky note was on the other side. All it read was, "call me." Jon recognized Alegra's handwriting and after taking the last cigarette, he tossed the pack, note and all, in the garbage. He thought for a moment about lighting it, but he decided against it. He had already been warned about smoking in the apartment before, and he tried to make it a habit of going outside to smoke now. Right now, though, going outside was not something he felt he should be doing.

He got up off the couch with a labored groan and walked to the bathroom. He looked himself over in the mirror. Bruises had shown up overnight on his neck in the shape of a handprint. He took his shirt off to check the rest of the damage. He expected a larger bandage to be covering his shoulder and arm. Luckily for Jon, only a small patch was taped over whatever wound was there. Ever so carefully, Jon removed the bandage on his shoulder. The bullet that struck him must have just grazed him. It was small enough that Alegra decided he only needed a few stitches. Nothing life-threatening. Just another scar to add to the collection he had been growing for a while.

Jon was used to fighting, but his own blood was something that he never really had much of a tolerance for. He figured he had panicked on seeing the blood and his adrenaline was flowing to the point of keeping him going until he felt safe enough to pass out. He wished he had a better tolerance for seeing it outside his body. Alegra and Caine used to tease him to get a tattoo or two to build it up.

A small chirp in the living room caught Jon's attention and pulled him away from the bathroom. A little light on his phone told him a message had come in for him.

After taping in the passcode to unlock the phone, the screen shot to life and a message from the school where he was supposed to be teaching filled the screen. It was chastising him about not showing up for class without informing them, again. Jon shrugged, typed back "Late research" and then shot a quick message to Megan. "Late night. Need coffee" and gave her his address. After a bit, a thumbs up emoji came back.

Jon decided cleaning the soot and dirt from last night off himself might be a good idea before Megan arrived. It appeared Alegra had tried to at least clean his face for him. The rest of him still looked like he had been rolling in the dirt.

He went back into the bathroom where a small cabinet sat in the corner. Jon opened it and pulled out a set of clothes. He had always called them his "rough night" clothes. He had them set aside so hc would not have to go hunting in his bedroom for anything clean. He set the clothes on the closed toilet seat cover and started the shower.

A quick shower had already made Jon begin to feel better. After toweling off and redressing, plus popping a few of his joints here and there, he was already feeling good as new. He opened the medicine cabinet and pulled out some makeup that he had bought for such occasions and started to cover up the damage on his neck. Satisfied with the results, Jon walked back to the living room and sat down on the couch.

Alegra had already emptied his pockets for him. The letter, now slightly crushed, sat on the table in front of him. Jon picked up the letter and looked it over. As he did he felt a strange hum emanating from the parchment. Jon furrowed his brow in confusion. That sort of feeling was not something he was expecting from a letter. Thinking it was best not to touch it, Jon set the letter back down and turned on the TV.

After about thirty minutes of a mindless afternoon game show, there was a knock at Jon's door. He stood up and answered it. Megan stood there with two large Styrofoam cups of coffee. Jon motioned her inside, and she followed him.

"Only been a week or so," Megan found the cup she labeled for Jon and handed it to him. She took a glance around. "And I'm already in the boss's apartment. Casting couch time to earn that promotion to an Angel huh?"

"Funny." Jon took a sip of the coffee. He found it slightly disappointing. "What's in this?"

"Cream and sugar," Megan explained. She was not sure if she had done anything wrong, but it was the same way she had got it for him before.

"Future note," Jon walked to the kitchen, opened a bottle of whiskey, and he poured some in. "Days I'm off? Cream, sugar, and whiskey. Helps with the aches and pains."

"Getting that old?" Megan laughed slightly.

"Got attacked by a vampire last night," Jon calm way of explaining this made it seem almost like a daily occurrence. He walked away from his kitchen area and rejoined Megan by the couch.

"Why?" Megan questioned. Jon gave a slight snicker at the idea that "why" was he first question and not one of confusion about what he said. She sounded like she was already getting used to her new life.

"I was robbing him." Jon took a sip of his spiked coffee. "I took that envelope on the table. Do me a favor and open it could you?"

Megan picked up the envelope and broke the seal with her finger. Jon ducked slightly as she did.

"What was that for?" Megan questioned, confused as to why Jon reacted that way.

"Did you feel how it was kind of vibrating slightly as you picked it up?" Jon sat back down on the couch next to Megan.

"Yeah?" Megan nodded, still confused.

"Great." Jon pointed to the door across from the bathroom. "Do NOT try and open it but go touch the door. It's my bedroom."

"It's kinda humming," Megan informed Jon as she gently touched it.

"It has a spell on it," Jon informed her. "There are only two people who can open that door. My wife and myself. If anyone other than those two people try and open it, a large explosion will rip from it and kill whoever tried."

"What you're saying is," Megan got visibly upset. "You just told me to open a god damn bomb?!"

"No," Jon shook his head. "Ok, not really…kind of? Yes. However, it was a very calculated risk. Whoever put that spell on the letter probably only put it on there against magic users, or maybe supernaturals. But there was something off with the vibrations. I'm not too keen on reading those vibrations, but I do know a little bit. If you feel my door again, it is a constant buzz. When you felt the letter, there was only a slight tick to it. It was almost unnoticeable if you didn't know what you were looking for, but it was there. The spell on that letter wasn't as strong. It's meant to scare people off, not actually go off. Which meant you probably could have opened it."

"What you're telling me," Megan calmed down. "Is you *potentially* handed me a god damn bomb. What would you have done if it went off?"

"Cleaned you up off my carpet," Jon explained as if it would just be a mild inconvenience for him. "Have to deal with a very pissed off demon, and maybe a few other people. Usual stuff. What does the bomb say?"

Megan glared at Jon. While she hated how aloof he was about the whole situation, something about his aloof attitude told her that he had everything under control. This was not a man who just flew by the seat of his pants, but he gave off the impression that he did for one reason or another. Calmed further by this revelation, Megan unfolded the envelope and saw a bunch of scribble marks all over it.

"I have no idea," Megan held the item up for Jon to see. "It's spaced out like writing, but I can't read it."

Jon took it from Megan and began pouring over it.

"Of course, you can't." Jon rubbed his chin. He looked closer and was apparently reading it. "It maguscript..."

"Ok," Megan rolled her eyes. "You just made that word up, like manuscript."

"Yeah," Jon smirked slightly. "I have no idea what it's called. They never told me. However, I can read it, or enough of it. I'm a little rusty. I had to translate a few of these in my time in The Library. It's a language mages used to use to communicate with each other. However, unlike Greek or cuneiform, there is no Rosetta Stone to translate it from. It's effectively a dead language, but it's one which serves a purpose."

"What does it say?" Megan asked, leaning over to see it closer.

"It says that whoever wrote this has such horrible handwriting that I can't read enough of it to make sense." Jon sighed. He set the letter down and scratched his head absentmindedly.

"So, we got nothing from it," Megan concluded. "You got your ass beat for nothing."

"Nope," Jon smiled big. "It confirmed something for me. I met our friend Grool last night. Turns out he was the owner of the strip club that Alegra, Caine and I got Miko from. He's the vampire."

"This Grool guy wrote the letter?" Megan asked as she saw Jon take a picture of the letter with his phone. He then tapped a few buttons on his phone and then turned it off and set it down.

"No," Jon shook his head. "He mentioned that his boss gave him some cool vampire powers before we fought. But it struck me as odd."

"Why's that?" Megan shrugged. "Bite and go right? Poof, instant vampire."

"No, if that were the case there would be about a million vampires running around," Jon sipped his coffee and sat back. "Now, I'm not too certain about vampires. I skipped that day of class. What I do know is that most legends state they drain a person and right before that moment of death, feed them their blood. Then you get another vampire."

"Ok," Megan was listening intently. "Still don't see an issue here."

"The club burned down after Alegra attacked Grool," Jon explained. "She tore off some of his flesh and set the cheap curtains on fire. Do you know one thing most undead creatures hate?"

"Gonna go out on a limb and say fire?" Megan suggested.

"Exactly," Jon grinned with how quickly Megan was catching on. To him it was a confirmation of his line of thought. "So how could a vampire enter a burning room to make another vampire? They wouldn't. Fire is supernaturally cleansing, and they're too flammable. This tells me two things. One; Grool's boss isn't a vampire. Two;

neither is Grool. Now, while I don't know much about vampires, I do know about magic. Two types of magic users can effectively heal someone from that state. The first are called 'Healers.' They deal with helping the sick and all that pious stuff. The others are 'Blood Mages.' Due to the 'evil' nature of their magics and the practices needed to get them, they were removed from The Library. Violence against normal people is against The Library's code. It also goes against a lot of supernatural laws. You hurt the normal people, and you get witch hunts. No mage in their right mind wants that again. Now, a healer would have healed Grool, no questions asked. However, they tend to get together in holy places; churches, faith-based hospitals, etc. So, our chances are quite slim it was one of them."

"Grool's boss is a blood mage?" Megan confirmed where Jon was going with all this.

"Precisely," Jon smiled big, amused at his conclusions. "And I just sent a member of The Library a picture of that letter to see if he knows who's handwriting it is. This region of Washington's mage population is rather small. There is a chance he can find out who it is, and if not, maybe he can decipher the letter."

"What do we do now?" Megan asked. "Wait?"

"I wait." Jon leaned back in his seat. "You have a date."

"Excuse me?" Megan raised an eyebrow.

"That guy you went to that game session with," Jon brought up the picture with the reptilian creature on it. "Did he tell you where it came from?"

"No," Megan shook her head. "I kind of bolted before he could. I thought he would make me delete the picture."

"Smart," Jon informed her. "A little birdy told me that whatever it is, it's either new, or it doesn't exist. So, what my birdy also told me is that it's probably a familiar.

"A familiar is a creature made of pure magic," Jon began to teach as he could see the term was unfamiliar to Megan. "Magic users and other supernatural things tend to use them as a slave."

"Got ya," Megan was grateful that her employer was a teacher and explaining things like this was second nature to him.

"You know what else our feathered friend told me?" Jon leaned closer to Megan. "Neither does Miko. You were right, she's not a nekomata; she's a neko-maymay, or whatever you called her. She's a familiar too. Familiars can have any sort of look or shape you want. A cat girl and a thing that looks like it came from a video game, in one town, is too big of a coincidence to not follow up on."

"What do you want me to do?" Megan asked, stunned by the amount of information Jon was giving her.

"Well," Jon checked his phone for any missed messages. One had come in from Alegra who was checking on him. Jon ignored it. "I think you need to make it up to him. Get a little closer. Figure out where that thing came from. You still have his number?"

"He's tried to contact me a few times," Megan admitted. "I've kind of ignored it. Don't have a habit of dealing with guys that thirsty."

"I have no idea what that means." Jon shook his head.

"He wants to fuck me," Megan sighed at having to explain things to the older man. "Bad."

"Well," Jon stood up, "pick up some rubbers. You may need them. That was a joke by the way."

"A really bad one," Megan informed him as she picked up her phone and sent a message. "Please don't ask me to do that again, even jokingly."

"No problem." Jon agreed remorseful of his failed attempt at a joke.

Megan's phone rang. She rolled her eyes slightly and mouthed "here goes." She answered the phone.

"Hi, Andy." Megan put on her best fake smile. Even though she knew he could not see her, she was always told it still came through in her voice. "Sorry, I was out of town and didn't get any reception. Huh? Oh yeah, doing research for Jon. Say, the reason I texted you was I felt bad about just ditching out on you the other night. Do you want to get coffee, my treat? Dinner? That sounds better. Poor college girl has to eat, right? Sushi? Uh sure, I can honestly say I've never had it, but I'll try anything once. Ok, tomorrow?"

Jon tapped her on the shoulder and mouthed Friday.

"Andy?" Megan continued. "Can we do Friday? Jon's being kind of a stickler about this project. That's better? Right, the game is tomorrow, I forgot. No, I can't make it. Sorry. Oh no, it's not the other guys. It's..."

Megan fumbled in her mind for a proper response.

"That I just kind of wasn't feeling it," Megan cringed as she said this, "but I want to still spend some time with you. Andy? You still there? Oh, there you are. Friday is good then? Great! Would you mind going to a show afterwards? A local band is playing and I kind of wanted to check them out. If you don't like it, we'll bounce. Sound good? Great! Seven for dinner. See you then."

Megan hung up the phone.

"Great, that will give me time to make a few plans," Jon began pacing as plans came together in his head. "And you have a big date to get ready for."

"You're paying for my date." Megan stayed seated. "You're paying for the show. If I'm going this far, I'm at least getting a good show out of it."

Jon sighed and pulled out his wallet. He pulled out a one-hundred-dollar bill and handed it to Megan. Megan stuffed it in her pocket.

"Let me know when you get word about what the story is," Jon rubbed his hands together excitedly then checked his phone again. "I've got some people to talk to."

Chapter 18

"Why am I still dealing with this Jon?" Steve sat at a table in the back corner of Misshapen. Jon sat to his left, and Caine sat to his right.

"Were you able to decipher that letter I sent you?" Jon asked and sipped on a beer.

"What letter?" Caine asked. Jon held up a finger to tell him to hold his thought.

"No," Steve gave Jon the bad news. "Whoever wrote that has a very poor grip on the language, and the nuances of writing it."

"It wasn't just me." Jon gave a sight of relief that his skills were not a rusty as he thought.

"What letter?" Caine asked again. Jon pulled out his phone and showed Caine a picture of the letter he had found earlier.

"I found this back at the strip club," Jon informed Caine. "I went back to see if there was anything else there.

If there was a vampire, there had to be a lair. I went to find it and did. I found that letter."

"And my hat," Alegra added to the conversation from the bar. She proudly sported the hat Jon brought back from the strip club.

"What do you mean back?" Steve threw in there. "You told me you were just around after it burned down."

Jon ignored the question as Caine chimed in.

"Why would you go into the lion's den?" Caine asked raising a naked eyebrow.

"Something was sitting wrong with me after meeting Malcolm," Jon began. "It was when we went into his little throne room. Did you notice anything about the torches on the wall?"

"I was too busy watching to make sure the predator in the room didn't lunge at you," Caine admitted.

"They were all electric," Jon pointed out to Caine. "Very well done, expensive fakes, but fake none the less. I didn't want to call it out at that time because it wasn't important. One thing I do know about vampires was confirmed there. Vampires hate fire."

"True." Steve agreed.

"Alegra," Jon turned to the bartender. "When you bit Grool, did he taste funny? Ashy like that thug?"

"No." Alegra furrowed her brow trying to remember. "None at all."

"Have you ever eaten vampire flesh before?" Jon asked. Alegra shook her head again. "But you were quick to point out when the thug tasted funny. I figure you might have done the same if Grool tasted funny too."

"I was more worried about getting out before the building burned down." Alegra began cleaning some glasses. "I might have later."

"Between that," Jon continued, "and what he told me…"

"You met Grool?" Caine questioned.

"Grool was the guy running the club," Jon informed him. "Back to what I was saying. Grool told me he got turned into a vampire. That was when it hit me. How could a vampire enter the room? It was on fire."

"Can you cut to the chase?" Steve was getting annoyed.

"I'm getting there." Jon drank from his beer. "A vampire couldn't enter a burning room, but a blood mage who can mend Grool could."

"A blood mage?" Steve got visibly upset. "In New Hancock?"

"It's the only thing that makes sense," Jon informed Steve. "That was how they found Alegra. The mage read and followed the hairs in the hat. On top of that. A mage has to be close to the club, or else Miko would have died like she almost did earlier. Now, a healer wouldn't want anything to do with this seedy business. A blood mage can use nearly all bodily fluids, blood is just the easiest way to explain it. Think about the amount of that there is in the place. They would be perfect to run it."

"Blood magics aren't illegal on their own," Caine reminded Jon. "Why are we sitting here?"

"These guys are out there hurting supernatural people," Jon got to the point. "They're running a damn slavery ring. We need to bring them down. We have evidence."

"I've already explained," Steve groaned. "Familiars aren't people. Miko is not a person. She doesn't have rights. She could be bought, sold, beat and slaughtered like its nothing."

173

"I can?" The group quickly turned to see Miko with wide sad eyes and a tray of drinks frozen in place.

"I…" Steve froze when confronted with his words. Alegra quickly rushed to the cat girl's side and took the tray of drinks from her. She set them on the table and then ushered her out of the room.

"Miko is…" Caine began after they left.

"Just roll with it, Caine," Jon shook his head, and angrily turned his attention to Steve. "Typical Library, something is fucked up, and you old assholes don't want to take the chance to help make things right."

"I know it seems wrong Jon," Steve tried to calm Jon who was getting visibly upset. "But there is nothing against any laws going on, The Library's or supernatural laws."

"He's right, Jon," Caine informed Jon. "Nothing wrong there. Knowing all this now, I don't know why I'm even sitting here. Had I known Miko was a familiar I would have put a stop to that whole adventure."

"I'm not needed here," Steve realized he had nothing to do with this conversation and began to get up. "You know, Jon. Had you stayed with us; you wouldn't be wasting anyone's time."

With that, Steve made a wave of his hand and a portal appeared. Steve began to walk through and stopped.

"Jon," Steve turned around. "Your heart is in the right place. Call me if I can do anything else for you."

With that Steve walked through the portal, and it closed behind him.

"Caine," Jon began. Caine held up a hand.

"I understand where you are coming from," Caine interrupted. "But look, we got Miko out of there. You're taking this too far. I wish I could be of more help. Why don't you all just lay low for a while and let this whole thing just blow over? I'm sure Grool and whoever this mage is will cut their losses eventually."

"There's a damn mage out there fucking with people," Jon protested. "Look at this."

Jon pulled the picture from the binder out on his phone and showed it to Caine.

"Where does it stop?" Jon asked. "They're already making plans for more."

"Then that's a magus issue and The Library already declined to help," Caine pulled a card out of his pocket and set it on the table in front of Jon. "This is my contact with the FBI. She handles mages. If they are hurting humans, then tell her what you found."

"Let me ask you a question." Jon stared at the card idly flipping it over and over in his hand. "A familiar is a creature kept around by magic, but they are only around to do their master's bidding. They have no real will of their own. When we took Miko out of that building, did you see any hesitation from her? Do you see any struggle in her trying to go back?"

"Jon..." Caine rubbed his head. He wanted to say something. Something to make his friend feel better about the situation, but he could not find the words. "I'm sorry, Jon. I've made my call."

"So," Jon nodded to himself tapping the card on the table. He pursed his lips deep in thought. The door closed as Caine left the bar. "I'm in this alone. Fine. Not the first time I've done that. I can do this."

"Jon," A hand touched Jon's shoulder. Jon looked up to see Alegra standing next to him. She then took a seat at the table next to Jon. "I'm still here. We will think of something, or just lay low like Caine said."

The two sat there in silence for a minute. Jon's mind going through all sorts of thoughts. He wanted to come up with a plan, but nothing came to him. Jon patted Alegra's hand that was sitting on the table as a way of thanking her for sticking with him in this.

The door to the bar slowly opened and slow, as nervous footsteps came across the hardwood floor...

Chapter 19

Megan leaned her head on the backrest of the bus. Nervously, she played with the holes in her fishnets. She mindlessly toyed with a hole she had torn in them earlier and then ripped it slightly larger. She had not gone all out on her outfit, but she hoped it was still enough to entice Andy and make him drop his guard trying to impress her.

The bus passed by a few restaurants before Megan pulled the stop cord. She was not a fan of sushi. It wasn't the taste; as she had eaten it plenty of times and had a fondness for unagi. It was just how overplayed it was done on first dates. She had always wondered if it was always the go-to because it was popular and seemed expensive enough to impress with, or if her choice in dates just were not that creative. She made a promise to herself not to even kiss someone good night if their first date was sushi.

Megan got off the bus and looked around the strip mall to see if her "date" had arrived yet. She pulled out her phone and texted Andy to see where he was. After a few moments, a text came back saying he was a few minutes out and to grab a table. Megan did not want to rush into this and texted back that she had not arrived yet either. She told him that she was running late and to have him get the table for them. She would be there shortly.

To be fair, she was not technically at the restaurant yet, Megan justified to herself. She had to make a quick pitstop first. She ducked down a nearby alley and pulled a metal flask out of the inner pocket of her leather jacket. She used the reflective surface to check her make-up, and then unscrewed the top and took a quick sip. The quick bite of whiskey burned going down, and with that, her inhibitions were being melted away.

"Can I get a sip of that?" A homeless man in the alley coughed out. Megan had not noticed him before.

"Huh?" Megan gasped slightly as she jumped slightly and moved her hand to a can of mace in her pocket. When she realized it was just a frail older gentleman, she let go of her grip and handed him the flask.

"Thanks." The man took a few gulps and screwed the top back on. "Pretty girl like you shouldn't be in an alley like this by herself."

"Eh," Megan shrugged as the man handed her the flask back. "If something happened to me over here, I would have an excuse to cancel this date I really don't want to be on."

"Want out?" The older man chuckled and gave her a friendly smile from behind a long unkempt beard. "Why? Might have a good time."

"I highly doubt that," Megan lamented. She wanted to explain why she was really on the date but decided she had to come up with a lie quickly. Telling him the truth might not be the best idea. "It was a blind date set up. He suggested sushi. I mean, seriously? Is it because I'm Japanese?"

"Gets guys ready for the smell to go south." The old homeless guy joked. Megan shared a laugh with him and felt her phone go off. She sighed and checked the messages. Andy had arrived and had been seated.

"Great," Megan groaned. "Here goes. Frankly, I would rather sit here and drink with you."

"You're young," The old man coughed out again and shook his head. "Should be out there making mistakes. Not sitting here with an old guy like me. I mean, if you're not into this guy, at least have some fun with it. You ain't ever going see him after this so, fuck it. Caring, not him, or if you want to do him too. Have some fun."

"You're right," Megan agreed. She was not sure if he was trying to make a point or if the loneliness of his lifestyle had begun to take a toll on his mental health. "Might as well enjoy myself."

Megan reached down and gave her drinking partner a quick hug. A small thanks to him for listening to her and sharing a drink. She then moved out of the alley and towards the front of the restaurant.

After she entered through the front door, a waitress greeted her at the mahogany looking counter. The place was dimly lit and decorated like a Japanese tea house. Megan told the waitress she was meeting someone, and the woman nodded. She then led Megan to the table where Andy was seated. He quickly stood up to pull out her chair for her, and then push her back in. She was trapped.

Megan could not help but notice Andy was overdressed. A button-up dress shirt and a tie. To top it all off, a trilby sat on his head. She knew deep down he would have called it a fedora, but she did not care. Try and have fun, she had to remind herself. Try and have fun and do not bolt after telling him you have to go to the bathroom.

"Hey," Megan gave her best fake smile to Andy. "Nice place."

"Found this place while looking for ramen in the area when I first moved out here." Andy recounted the story. "They don't serve it though."

"You didn't check a menu online?" Megan questioned. Good, she told herself, keep the conversation going. It will make things go by quicker.

"I didn't think about it." Andy shrugged. Poor guy, Megan continued in her head. He was trying. She had almost felt bad about what she was doing to him. Almost.

"It happens." Megan unfolded a napkin and put it on her lap. "You found a good sushi place. I would call it a happy accident."

"I've never actually eaten here." Andy quickly explained.

"Then how do you know," Megan began teasing Andy, "you brought me to a good place?"

"I mean…" Andy began to visibly sweat. "It's got good reviews and and and…"

"Andy," Megan changed her tone to a more comforting one. "I'm just joking. I'm sure this is fine."

"Ok good," Andy seemed to calm down. The waitress came by and asked for their drink order. Andy went with cola, and Megan just stuck with the water that was poured for her. "I mean we could have gone somewhere else."

"Nah," Megan shook her head. "I'm used to being treated to a burger and fries. It's nice to have somewhere fancier now and then."

"I can do fancy." Andy tipped his hat. "I'm the kind of gentlemen that can do fancy quite well."

"I can see," Megan played along and tried not to cringe. "What do you do for work that allows something like this?"

"I actually," Andy started. He had a hard time finding words. Whatever was about to come out of his mouth was either going to be a lie, or embarrassing. She couldn't wait for his answer. "Don't work. My parents won't let me and tell me to focus on my studies."

Embarrassing. Megan was mildly amused by this answer, however, she felt it gave her an opening.

"So how can you afford this?" Megan brought the teasing voice back out. "Your mom paying for it?"

"No," Andy quickly changed his tone. He realized he said something he should not have if he wanted the date to go well. "I mean, I have a job. It's just…"

"It's just what?" Megan pushed. The waitress returned to take their order. Megan cursed in her head. This gave Andy a bit of breathing room. Both made their orders.

"Unagi?" Andy questioned. "That's eel."

"It's pretty good." Megan took a drink of water and leaned forward on the table. "The eel sauce on there makes it divine."

Megan noticed her slip up. She had told Andy she had never had sushi before, and here she was giving him advice on it.

"Huh," Andy swirled the ice in his cola. "Makes my teriyaki chicken seem a little boring."

Megan held in a sigh of relief that he did not catch it, or that he didn't care.

"You like what you like." Megan shrugged. The subject had been changed. She lost her chance to press him about his job.

"Yeah," Andy smiled slightly, "that is true."

Both remained quiet. Megan had no problem with awkward silences, she considered going to the bathroom to wait peacefully for the food, but she thought better of it. She did not want Andy to get the idea that she was not interested in spending time with him. She was not, but she did not want him to get that idea.

"I wanted to apologize again," Andy started. "About yelling at you the other night."

"You yelled at me?" Megan thought back to the other night. Wait, she mentally questioned, did he think he was yelling at her? Was that his yelling?

"Oh," Andy stammered slightly as he backtracked, "I mean, I just didn't want knowledge of Shorty getting out. At least that's what the woman told me after I summoned my first creature."

Megan could not help letting her eyes grow big, and she froze stunned. Was this happening? Did this guy just blurt out the information she thought was going to take her all night to get out of him? She could leave now and have accomplished her mission. However, she planned, if she stayed maybe she could get more out of him.

"You summoned him?" Megan lowered her voice. "How?"

"I can't really explain it," Andy was just opening up. Was he trying to use this knowledge to impress her? "It's kind of this magic thing I do."

"Magic?" Megan asked. She leaned in to give a look of genuine interest. "You can summon little green men?"

"I bought this book at an old bookstore." Andy began. "It had passages on how to summon things based on your imagination. Thinking it would be fun, I gave it a try. I never thought it would work. I summoned, like, some sort of cat girl."

"Where is she?" Megan asked. She did not recall seeing anything like that at Andy's house.

"I..." Andy went quiet. He looked away from his date. Obvious shame came across his face. "I had no idea what to do with her. She was friendly, but not what I was looking for. I mean she was a cat girl, not a cat girl. You know what I mean? She didn't look right. Awfully friendly and helpful. Figured she would make a great stripper..."

That was where his mind instantly went? Megan spat in her mind. She tried to not let it show that she was getting angry as he was telling his story. She needed to hear everything from him.

"Heard about this club that specialized in freaks," Andy continued. "I found it, and I talked to the owner. He said his boss might be interested. I met her, and she explained a lot to me. Told me I could use magic, and that there was a lot of people like me. She told me that if I continued to make these creatures for her, that she would introduce me to more people. That they would teach me how to better use and harness my powers."

"You made Shorty for her?" Megan filled in some blanks.

"I did," Andy looked down at his drink. He felt the need to hide as his nerves started to get to him as the memories of the story came back. "She got upset and told me that she needed human things. She told me not to come back unless I had something like that, and that if I screwed up again..."

Food arrived. That was fine, Megan figured. It sounded like Andy was growing uncomfortable but kept going because it seemed to make her pay attention to him.

The two ate in relative silence. Megan changed the subject and occasionally brought up their classes and what it was like to work for Jon. Soon, the meal was finished.

"So," Andy began as he looked down at the check. He pulled out a cloth wallet with a symbol from the role-playing game he ran, printed on it. He pulled out some cash and put the money on the table. "What's this concert we're going to?"

Fuck, Megan cursed in her head. She had forgotten about inviting him to the concert. She had planned for this to take longer and a few drinks to get the information out of him, but with him giving it up voluntarily, she was trapped. She checked her phone for the time, or a text from Jon to get her out of this. There was nothing and there was plenty of time to get to the show. It might also be a good place to lose him though, Megan planned.

"It's a psychobilly show," Megan explained.

"I've never heard of it," Andy confessed, slightly ashamed. Megan did not expect him to know about it, or any of the bands. Normally she had no problem introducing someone to it, but not this guy. If she could get more out of him as the night went on then continuing things was bullet she would have to take.

"Take that old fifties rockabilly sound, and cross it with punk," Megan explained. "Now run it through a haunted house, and you have psychobilly."

"Sounds interesting," Andy pondered what that might sound like. "Should we take my car or yours?"

"I don't drive," Megan shook her head. "We'll take yours."

Andy looked nervous as he looked around for parking. The concert venue he was expecting was just a ratty, dive bar. The neighborhood was not even that safe this time of night.

"You're sure this is the place?" Andy asked nervously.

"I've been here a million times." Megan confirmed the location for him.

"It's a bar," Andy explained his realization. "Are they going to let us in?"

"It's fine," Megan felt like rolling her eyes but needed him to feel comfortable. "They'll check our ID's at the door, along with the ticket. They'll mark your hand to show you're underage, and then let you in. It's fine."

Andy parked the car and nodded. He climbed out and took a deep breath. Megan had already marched across the street and was waiting patiently for him. He quickly scurried across the empty street while holding his hat in place.

Quite a few people stood outside the bar, all dressed in black. The men were either in band shirts or punk gear with a million patches. Many of the women were either dressed the same way or in dresses with haircuts that Andy had only seen in a John Travolta musical. The smell of all the cigarettes going at once started to make him nauseous as he closed in on the group.

"Hey," A voice piped up from one of the men. A guy in blue jeans and vest with its fair share of patches made his way over to the two of them. "Ghoulie, was wondering if you were going to show up tonight."

"I wasn't going to miss a new group coming into town," Megan called back to the man Andy could only describe as tall and handsome. Everything Andy was not. She then ran up to him and he lifted her in a big hug. Megan realized that Andy was suddenly feeling emasculated and brought him closer to her.

"Who's this?" The guy looked Andy up and down. He was obviously trying to get a feel for the younger man. Something that, though Andy tried to hide it, obviously made him uncomfortable.

"This is my date, Andy," Megan introduced the two. The guy stuck his cigarette between his lips and reached out to shake Andy's hand. Nervously, Andy reached back. "Andy, this is Dan. He's a good friend of mine."

"Oh." Andy grew quiet.

"Don't worry," Dan laughed big. "Not *that* good of a friend."

"Oh," Andy perked up a bit. "I didn't…"

Both Dan and Megan chuckled slightly. Megan reached into her jacket and pulled out the flask from earlier.

"Drink for a drag?" Megan shook the flask.

"Deal." Dan traded his cigarette for the flask. He unscrewed the lid and took a big swig. Megan took a deep drag of the cigarette. Dan tried to hand the flask to Andy. He waved it off.

"I'm underage," Andy explained.

"So?" Dan scoffed and gave a slight smirk. "So is Ghoulie."

"Ghoulie?" Andy questioned as he looked over at Megan.

"It's an old nickname from high school," Megan explained. "Some stuck up bitch gave it to me as an insult. I knocked her front tooth out. No one used it as an insult again, but it just kind of stuck. Still have her tooth back home."

"She's a bit of a firecracker." Dan took another drag of the cigarette and then put an arm around Andy, "I'd watch my ass if I was you."

"I will." Andy kind of felt himself squirm at the man's touch. He was not sure what was making him uncomfortable, but he knew he wanted the guy to take his arm off him.

"Hey," Megan caught Andy's attention. "Let's head on in. See you in there, Dan."

Megan grabbed Andy's arm and pulled him inside. She pulled a couple of slips of paper out of her jacket pocket and handed it to a ticket taker seated on a stool right inside the door. The ticket taker scanned the tickets and motioned for the two to head further. A bouncer stopped them next. Megan pulled out her ID and handed it to the bouncer and held out her arm. The bouncer put a wristband around it and motioned for her to go in further. Andy pulled out his. The bouncer looked at it, then at Andy, and then pulled out a marker and marked Andy's hand with an "X." Andy did not question it and followed Megan deeper into the place.

"I thought this was a bar," Andy admitted as Megan led him to a dark room with nothing but a stage on one side and a bar at the back of the room.

"It is," Megan explained as she pulled the two of them through the crowd and closer to the stage. "It's also a concert hall. If you go upstairs, they have a music shop. I'll take up there after the show if it's still open. Be right back."

Megan then disappeared back into the crowd and left Andy to his own devices. He looked around and saw more people of various ages, all older than himself, that looked like the crowd outside. Andy could not help but feel very out of his element.

It was not long before Megan returned with a cheap beer in a large can. Andy could already smell the whiskey on her breath earlier, and now it was stronger than when she left him alone.

"I thought you were a minor?" Andy questioned. The noise and inexperience of the crowd started to trigger a bit of social anxiety. He was not thinking clearly.

"The ID I gave the bouncer says I'm not," Megan chuckled and Andy's naivete and took a big drink. "So, I'm not right now. Right now, I'm twenty-two."

"Hmm..." Andy mused as he looked around and noticed all the guys around the place. Each one, he felt, was better looking and more like someone Megan would rather be with than him. He was ready for her to ditch him for one at any moment. "So, how do you know Dan?"

"Danny boy?" Megan pointed him out on the other side of the floor talking to some woman. She put her arm around Andy's shoulders. She did not want to drive him away, and the alcohol was making spending time with him easier. "A friend introduced us. The we got fucked up and had a three-way. Good shit. We kept running into each other at shows, and so we just became concert buddies."

"I see." Andy tried to not sound disappointed.

"Oh, don't worry about him," Megan took another drink. "We decided we were better friends than anything else. So, we cut out the fucking, and just kind of hang. Unless we are alone at the end of the night and have had waaayyy too much to drink. So, you had better keep me entertained."

"I can do that," Andy lied.

"I bet." Megan took off her leather jacket and handed it, and the beer, to Andy as the lights began to dim a bit and the opener hit the stage. Within moments, a bunch of people began slamming into each other as the aggressive punk sound came flooding from off from the stage. Andy quickly lost sight of Megan as he was knocked to the ground by a bigger guy who had hit him, hard. The two got tangled and the man fell on top of him.

Andy began to feel panic. He had heard stories of people getting stomped in these mosh pits. However, the reality was much different. A few guys created a barrier around the two on the floor, and the people at the perimeter picked the two of them up. Another arm grabbed Andy and pulled him further away from the craziness.

"Over here, coat rack." The voice belonged to Dan from earlier.

"Huh?" Andy was still loopy from the unexpected hit he took earlier.

"Stay behind the rim," Dan instructed after pulling him close so they could hear each other over the music. "They will keep those guys in there."

"Thanks," Andy breathed a sigh of relief. Dan took the beer from him and took a swig. "I think I spilled a little bit on Meg's jacket when I fell."

"She ain't gonna care," Dan smiled. "Until she hears you call her Meg. She might add your tooth to her collection."

"Right," Andy looked around. He realized that he had probably lost all interest from Megan. He was not as good looking as these other guys. He was not brave or strong enough to enter that pit. He did not even have a fake ID to let him drink at the bar. "Hey, I got to go to the bathroom. Can you hold these for me?"

"Sure." Dan took the jacket from Andy. "No worries."

"Thanks." Andy meekly gave his appreciation and quickly headed to the bathroom he saw by the front door. He stepped inside, looked at himself in the dirty mirror, washed his hands, and then instead of heading back to the concert hall, he took a turn and went outside.

He was not too far from his car when the sound of running footsteps came up from behind him.

"Hey," Megan called out. "You ok?"

"Yeah," Andy just stared down. He didn't want the young woman to see the look of defeat on his face. "I just..."

"Sorry," Megan smiled as sweetly as she felt she could right now. Andy must have felt over his head, cowardly, and defeated for having lost his date tonight. He never had her, but she had to make sure that he did not realize that. "I know I can come off a bit strong and a bit much. Why don't you come back in, enjoy the show?"

"I think you might have more fun if you didn't feel you had to babysit me." Andy admitted solemnly.

"Maybe we'll take it a little slower next time." Megan felt she had lost. She had the information she needed but might need him for more. Maybe to lead her and Jon to whoever originally bought Miko. Fuck it, she thought, desperate times called for desperate measures.

"Next time?" Andy was confused.

"It's not all the time I get treated like a lady." Megan leaned in and took the side of his face in her hand, and gently kissed him. A little longer than she would have liked, but at least there was no tongue involved.

"Next time." Andy was mesmerized.

"Good," Megan smiled. "I'm going to go back in. I'll find my way home from here. Done it before while much drunker. I'll text you when I get home. Don't worry about me."

Still semi-mesmerized, Andy got into his old white car, started the car, and drove off. Megan watched to make sure the car was out of sight before returning to the bar. Dan met her at the door with her jacket.

"Looks like your date took off." Dan pointed out, handing Megan her jacket back.

Without a word, she put the jacket back on. She then reached in the pocket and pulled her flask back out. She took a big mouthful, swished it around and spit it on the ground. She then took another, bigger pull on the flask, closed it and put it back in her pocket.

"Thank Christ," Megan spat. "Your car close?"

"Of course," Dan pointed to the direction where he had parked. "I'm sober enough to drive like you asked. You were being cryptic on the phone earlier. Everything cool?"

"Work stuff," Megan replied. "Everything you saw had to do with work. Can you give me a lift to another bar?"

"No problem," Dan was confused, but he went along with what Megan was requesting. He led the two of them to a black sedan a block away. "Are you going to fill me in? That guy wasn't your type."

"I already said work stuff," Megan explained. "Besides, you wouldn't believe me if I told you."

"You just kissed Mr. Fedora good night," Dan snickered to himself as he unlocked the vehicle. "I would believe just about anything right now."

"Guy stirred up some shit," Megan climbed in and buckled herself in the car. "My boss has me trying to figure out how. I'll tell you where you are going from here. You pretty much take Central Park Ave."

Dan flipped on his car's lights and drove off.

Megan was silent for the entire trip. Aside from giving directions every now and then, Megan just stared out the window. She could have tried to text Jon and see if she could meet him at his apartment. She then remembered that he would not be home. Jon had told her he had a meeting tonight to see if he could get some help with stopping this blood mage from continuing a modern slave trade. She was not sure if it was all she had to drink tonight, or if she was coming to terms with her future. She knew where she needed to go.

"That's it," Megan informed her driver. "Just drop me off by the door."

"In this neighborhood?" Dan looked around. "I'm coming with you."

"No," Megan refused his offer as Dan pulled the car off to the side and pressed the hazard flashers. "It's cool. See that guy walking around the corner. The tall guy in the suit? He's a friend of mine. Anything happens, I'll just call out his name and he'll be right there."

"He looks kind of breakable." Dan squinted, staring into the darkness trying to get a better look at Caine turning the corner.

"Thanks for backing me up in case things went south with Andy," Megan unbuckled her seatbelt. She completely ignored the comment Dan had just made. "Go back and enjoy the show. I didn't pay for your ticket for you to be worrying about me out here."

"If you need anything…" Dan informed Megan as she climbed out of the car.

"I'll give you a call," Megan finished the sentence for Dan.

Megan shut the door behind her, and Dan's car began to move away into the dark of night. She stared at the entrance to Misshapen. Whit did not sit in her normal spot just inside the door, and the lights were up too bright for the bar to be "open." Maybe they were cleaning up after a long night.

Megan began to head to the door and something in her made her stop. Everything she had seen those many nights before shot back into her mind. She froze. She took a few quick breaths and tried to calm herself. She wanted to help. She wanted to be part of this team. To do that she would need to face everything she had been avoiding.

"You don't have to go in," Caine's familiar voice came from behind Megan. She looked up to see him standing behind her. At first, she was confused as she had seen him walking off around the corner in the opposite direction. As she thought about it, and everything she had seen up this point, she just decided to let it go. She was beginning to accept that the world around her had become a lot more different than she had known.

"Miko's counting on me," Megan informed the tall man. "So is Jon."

"Once you go in that door," Caine's voice was flat. Megan was not sure if he was trying to change her mind or if he was just stating facts. "You won't be able to change your path. You will become a vigilante. Just like Jon, and just like Alegra."

"I thought you were on the same team as Jon?" Megan turned to face Caine.

Caine silently shook his head.

"Our paths cross." Cain's blank expression as he explained this was slightly unnerving. "Sometimes we help each other, but we are not on the same side. Some of us must represent law and order in this dark world. Help keep the sheet over the eyes of the public."

Megan looked at the door again. Something in her peripheral vision caught her eye. Megan looked up to see Miko as she stared out the window. Even in the darkness, Megan could see in her bright eyes shine, and that something was wrong. Megan tried to wave, but there was no return greeting. The cat woman just stared out into the night sky. Lost in thought, lost in concern.

"Is she alright?" Megan asked Caine.

"She's a familiar," Caine put his hand on Megan's shoulder as he explained all this to her. "Abandoned and sold by her creator, abused by her buyer, and now just realizing she is nothing more than a piece of property. I would venture a guess and say no."

"Aren't you going to help her?" Megan's gaze never left the window.

"No…" Caine sounded like he wanted to say more but was interrupted.

"Then I will." Megan shook Caine's hand off her shoulder, and with a new sense of determination, marched to the door of Misshapen. She froze again. This time she shook the visions from her head. This was a path she wanted to walk. She may not be ready to face the world she was about to walk into, but it was now or never.

Megan slowly opened the door. She did not know what she was going to walk into. Was the stench still going to be there? The blood stained into the hardwood floor? She slowly and cautiously made her way through the entryway and turned the corner. Jon sat at a table on the side of the room. He stared blankly. He was noticeably lost in the beer in front of him. Alegra had her hand on his back as if to comfort him.

"Hey," Megan waved at both Jon and Alegra. She continued to walk closer to them and took a seat at the table where Caine sat earlier. She pulled her flask out of her jacket and put it in front of Jon. "This time I forgot the coffee."

"What are you doing here, kid?" Alegra questioned. It was easy to tell it was more out of genuine curiosity than a threatening question. Alegra herself was not even sure how Megan was able to come back after the gruesome sight she witnessed. She also was not sure if she could forgive herself for losing control and being the cause of it.

"I've been helping Jon," Megan informed her. "He had a theory about where Miko came from or at least a lead."

Jon reached out and opened the flask. He went for a drink but found it empty. He smiled slightly and handed it back to Megan. She shrugged and left it on the table.

"What did you find?" Jon asked.

"He admitted it," Megan leaned in, putting her elbows on the table. "I guess he thought it would impress me

194

or something. He said he sold her to someone and was told to keep doing it. He created Shorty after that. He told me he met with a woman that rejected the creature. She told him to create something better or she was going to expose him. I figure he got scared and never made anything after that. So, what's the plan, boss?"

"The plan is," Alegra jumped in. "You're going home. You don't need to be mixed up in all this. You could be hurt or killed getting involved in this."

Megan had not thought of that. She froze for a second. This was the second time her mortality was being thrown in her face. She wanted to take a deep breath, but all she could do was let the alcohol in her system crack half a smile.

"Good thing," Megan leaned back in her chair, "I've got a kick-ass, flesh-eating demon on my side then, huh?"

Alegra cocked an eyebrow and let a jagged, pointy-toothed smirk escape. As monstrous, and ferocious, the teeth made Alegra look, Megan could not help herself. All the stories she had heard. All the horror movies she had seen. Not even the violence she witnessed firsthand. The woman before her now was the same woman that had offered a ham sandwich on the first night they met. All it took was seeing that smirk to remind her that this woman was still a friend.

Jon stood up and reached for his keys in his pocket.

"Well," Jon slid his chair back into place at the table. "Looks like I have to come up with a plan. Alegra, I'll be in touch. Megan, come on. I'll give you a lift home."

Megan looked around as the two exited the bar. Caine was nowhere to be seen. Megan followed Jon to his car. She looked up at the window Miko was sitting in earlier and saw nothing. Alegra stood in the doorway of the bar, watching the two get in the vehicle. As soon as the engine was started, she reached up and pulled down the shutter.

"I honestly think you made her night," Jon chuckled. "She likes you. Seeing you be comfortable around her again means a lot of her."

"Yeah," Megan nodded. "I think so too. After everything is quiet and this is all said and done, I think I have an idea that will make her even happier."

"Oh?" Jon's interest was piqued as he opened the door to his car and climbed in. Megan did that same and buckled herself in. "Fill me in."

Chapter 20

A week had passed. Jon had held a meeting with Megan and Alegra to go over the plan. It was time they made their move. Time to meet the bad guy in all this. Time to face off with the blood mage, and make sure no one else was coming for Miko.

Megan thought she would have second guesses about doing all this. She figured she would back out as soon as she realized the danger. There was no quitting, however. There was not even a second thought. It was time to execute.

The young woman pulled the stop cord on the bus and after the large vehicle came to a complete stop, she got off. The suburban neighborhood was quiet. If everything went as planned, no one in the area would be any wiser that something supernatural was about to happen.

A quick look around confirmed to Megan that nothing unexpected was going to jump out at her that night. Megan knocked on Andy's front door and waited patiently for it to open. She had contacted him a few days after the two's first "date." He was quick to agree to have her come over for their second one.

"Hi, Meg," Andy's mother greeted her. Megan had to grin and bear it. She hated being called Meg. Certain people could get away with teasing her about it, but the woman in front of her was not one of those people. Megan had to remind herself that this was probably going to be the last time she saw the woman and that causing a scene this close to the endgame was not something she needed.

"Hi," Megan smiled sweetly behind the now stewing hatred. "I'm supposed to be meeting Andy here. Is he ready for me?"

Megan had no idea if what she said had any meaning. Meeting someone for a date at their parent's place was not something she had ever planned to do. Anything she might have considered "fun" would be right out the window. Luckily, Andy informed her that his parents were good about giving him space and letting him be an adult. They had plans to go out that night, and Andy had told them he and Megan just planned to spend the night watching a movie or two and eating pizza. Megan hoped everything would go down as planned before whatever movie she had to suffer through would be put on.

"He's upstairs in his room." Andy's mother stepped aside letting Megan into the house. "He said to send you up when you got in."

"Thanks," Megan stepped inside. She kept her boots on and headed up the stairs. She gave a quick knock on the door Andy had led her to before.

"Go get the door, Shorty," Andy's voice responded. A strange gurgling and squealing sound came closer to the door. Megan stood there patiently. A few more seconds passed, and footsteps came to the door. Andy opened it with a grumble.

"Doesn't listen well," Megan smiled as Andy opened the door. "Does he?"

"No," Andy glared at the creature. He then greeted Megan with a quick kiss. She was unprepared and just let it happen. It probably gave off the wrong message to him for this job, but Megan did not care. "Uh, why don't you take a seat on the bed. I'm just about to go on a raid with my guild. You can see my awesome warlock skills."

"That sounds awesome." Megan hoped her feigned interest hid her lie well.

Megan sat on the bed and looked around the room. She was searching for the book Andy had told her he bought. It was only a matter of time before the small reptilian creature climbed on the bed with her. Without a word it just stared at her, silently. Megan did nothing but stare back. The creature shot its tongue out and licked its eyeball.

"I can't do that one," Megan giggled, "little dude."

The creature held its arms up. Megan again just stared at it. She had no idea what it wanted. It let out a shrill cry and moved its arms up and down.

"Andy!" A male voice came from downstairs. "Shut that damn thing up!"

"I don't know what it wants, dad!" Andy shouted back. "I don't speak weird, midget, reptile."

Megan just guessed what the creature wanted. She stood up and picked the creature up and rested him on her hip, just like one would a child. Shorty wrapped its arms around her and nuzzled its head against her chest.

"I think he just wanted to be held." Megan quietly informed Andy. She looked at the creature. It seemed extremely comfortable in its new position. The young woman could not help but find cuteness with how ugly the thing was.

"Whatever," The male voice yelled back. "We're leaving. So just deal with it."

Megan bounced Shorty on her hip and chuckled a bit seeing it do the closest to what she would consider smiling. Figuring it was having fun, she danced a little with it and bent over to do a little dip. The sound the thing made was a much more calm and happy sounding coo. She then walked over to Andy, who was staring intently into the computer.

"Say 'hi' to daddy," Megan teased.

"Get that thing away from me," Andy replied uninterested. He did not even turn to face them. "I'm seriously trying to pay attention. Besides, if I get too attached it will be harder to sell him when I find a buyer."

Megan did not know what to say. The more time she spent around Andy the more she did not want anything to do with him. At first, she figured he was a naïve kid who had no idea what he had got mixed up in, but now she realized he didn't even care to learn. She felt worse for Shorty on her hip than for what she was about to do to Andy.

"What does he eat?" Megan's curiosity got the better of her about Shorty.

"I dunno," Andy replied curtly. Megan looked over at the screen and could only guess that due to his change in attitude, he was losing or something. She was not very well versed in video games. Her brother was, and could probably explain what was going on, but she had no idea.

"You and your family live here your whole life?" Megan began exploring the room again.

"Yeah." Andy was not paying attention to her. Megan considered messing with the poor boy and reaching down to grab his crotch to see what he would do. She decided that might cause him to ejaculate and then he would not be putty in her hands. Right now, that was what she needed. She did not doll herself up for him not to be easily led.

"I'm gonna put you down for a second," Megan told Shorty. She could hear the garage door open and close. "I got to take my jacket off, getting kind of warm in here."

Megan set Shorty back on the bed. It continued to dance and twirl on its own, still having fun. Megan took off her jacket revealing the lowest cut top she could find at the store. She hated it but had to admit that it was kind of fun dressing for attention. She might have to do it more often.

The young woman looked out the window. Jon's car pulled up to the curb about a block down the street. It looked like everything was in position.

"Mind if I open the window?" Megan asked. "It's a little stuffy in here."

"Yeah, sure." Andy again responded, completely uninterested in Megan.

Megan opened the window. With that the scent of old soda and stale chips left the small bedroom slowly.

"Ah, that breeze feels nice." Megan leaned on the sill. She had purposefully not put a bra on and a bit of the chill in the air had given her chest one more weapon to use to keep the boy under her spell.

"Fuck!" Andy exclaimed and threw the headset he had been wearing. Shorty quickly jumped off the bed and grabbed it, put it on, and started babbling into it.

"You ok?" Megan faked concern.

"Our slowtard battery let our healer run out of mana," Andy complained, "and he let our DPS die and we got wiped."

Megan had no idea what any of that meant but figured it was not good.

Andy turned around to get his headset back from Shorty who had left to a different room of the house. However, when he turned around from the computer, the woman leaned against his desk made him forget all of that.

"Hi," Andy could not think. Megan had seen that face before and knew where all the blood from his brain had gone.

"Hi." Megan sarcastically waved.

"Hi," Andy repeated.

"We've already done that part." Megan reminded the young man in front of her.

"I'm sorry," Andy pointed at the computer. "I just got…"

Megan had to take his attention away from the game and fast. She took his hands and put them on her hips.

"I can tell you're pretty new at this," Megan gave an amused chuckle. "Andy, this is the next proper move."

"Got ya." Andy's mind was officially gone. Two nipples making themselves known through Megan's shirt were now his focal point.

"Why don't you tell your little friends," Megan leaned down closer to the boy in the chair, "you're going to be tied up for a minute or two."

Andy did not say anything. He turned to the computer and just hit a few keys. He turned back around and stood up. Megan just gave her best sultry look and sat back down on the bed. She crossed her legs, giving Andy just the tiniest peek of what was under her skirt. Not enough for him to see anything, but enough for him to want to see more. She leaned back slightly, giving herself a much more enticing "come hither" vibe.

She was terrible at this, and she knew it. Lucky for her, her "victim" in this case was worse. Normally, she never had to put this much effort into dealing with a guy. A few drinks, a direct come on, and she was getting something that night. For Andy though, she needed to lead this guy around the city by a certain body part. To do this, she had change who she was as to not almost lose him like the first time.

Luckily for her, a certain demon was happy to give her tips on how to trap her prey.

Andy stood up and moved closer to her. He put his hands on the bed, trapping Megan between them. He leaned in to kiss her again, but she moved away.

"Tsk tsk." Megan waved a finger. Alegra's lessons rang in her head again. Give him a little but make him work for more. It was a tactic she used when she danced to get bigger tips out of fewer spectators. "Now, where would our fun night be if we rushed things?"

"Good point." Andy collected himself and freed Megan. She let out an inner sigh of relief. Had he forced himself on her, she could have fought the scrawny guy off. The downside is that everything this far would be lost, or she would have to give in to his whims to keep everything going. Neither option was acceptable for her. "Hungry?"

"I had a better idea," Megan stood up and walked around the room a bit, she made her way to a bookshelf closer to the floor. She bent over at the waist to give Andy a better view. Again, something else she had practiced with Alegra. The stretch was already killing her legs, and her boot's heels were not helping her feet feel the best either. "Where is that book you were telling me about?"

"Here." Andy scurried around and reached under his mattress. He pulled out a dusty, old leather-bound book. "Why?"

Megan put on her best wicked smile and took the book from Andy. She sat down in his computer chair and began flipping pages.

"You know I do a lot of occult research for Dr. Bringer, right?" Megan did not peer up from the book. Sexy smart she told herself. Not a tactic from Alegra, but she figured what guy could not resist a little bit of brains. "I've been researching the writings of a few older mystics. Ever hear of a man named Alister Crowley?"

Andy shook his head. Megan closed the book to look at the guy sitting on the bed.

"Alister Crowley used to perform rituals," Megan explained. Jon had told her to bring this up if the conversation allowed it while watching Alegra give what he had deemed "sexy lessons" to his employee. "One of the things that he always talked about was how much magical energy was in sex and sexual tension. So, I was thinking, we skip the movie, we skip the pizza, and we move on to something a little more *satisfying*. There is already enough tension in the air that I'm sure whatever you summon from this little book could be ever so…filling. Don't you agree?"

Andy could not say a word. He just nodded, dumbfounded, and aroused.

"I saw that look in your eye when I mentioned that Dan and I had had a three-way," Megan cooed as she leaned back in her chair, and gently arched her back, giving Andy more to take in. "I'm not dressed like this to just to watch a movie. Let's say we summon something from that book, and you, me and it, make some of those wicked little fantasies come true?"

"Yes." A squeak was Andy could muster.

Andy took the book and sat on the floor. He quickly found the page that he had used a few times to summon both Shorty and Miko.

"What…" Andy stammered. "What should we summon?"

"There's a demon," Megan explained as she sat across from him on the floor. It was time to turn up the heat. She sat with her legs folded in front of her but left a small crack between them, giving Andy a full view of "the promised land." "Called a succubus. They are said to be very sexual demons. Enough to drive any man wild and sell his soul for one night. Since ours won't be real, there won't be any danger. What do you say?"

"Umm..." Andy flipped through the book. The voices of a man and woman softly arguing could be heard outside the window. Andy snapped out of Megan's charms. "What was..."

Megan threw herself at Andy. Her lips pressed against his. She gently used her mouth to lead Andy to open his and slipped her tongue into his mouth and began to explore it. All she could think was whatever he ate earlier tasted horrible and that he needed to brush his teeth.

"Let's get that demon." Andy softly spoke as the two parted.

Megan was surprised as Andy just sat there reading the passages to himself. She expected a lot more pomp and circumstance to the whole thing.

"Shouldn't there be more?" Megan asked wondering why there was no prep work being done. "Candles, chalk outlines, anything?"

"The book says that a lot of the candles and all that is for the mood." Andy refuted the thought. This was his time to impress her with his knowledge of the magical arts. They set the stage so to speak. They can help, but they are not needed. The mind's eye is usually all you need for this spell, and as a dungeon lord, I believe my mind's eye is strong enough."

"Do you ever use your mind's eye when you think of me?" Megan was more interested in the information than in Andy's boasting. However, a little ego boost for herself was never a bad thing.

"Uh..." Andy had no idea how to answer that. He just turned red and continued to read the passage. He felt comfortable understanding how to do the spell again and handed the book to her. "If we want her to be under both our command, we need to do the spell together."

"Fine," Megan took the book. "Don't answer my question. With how red you turned; I already have my answer."

Megan looked over the passages.

"Your book is wrong." Megan pointed out knowingly.

"I've got it to work before," Andy protested, "twice."

"For one person performing the spell," Megan pointed to the page. She didn't know if what she was pointing to had any relevance. She leaned down to give Andy something to look at other than what she was pointing at. "However, for two people you need a phrase to speak together to combine your wills. It was something I read in Crowley's works."

"Ok, what words would you suggest." Andy fell right into the trap. He had no idea she was making all this up as she went.

"The three best magic words known to man," Megan imparted her knowledge on the young man. "Klaatu Barada Nikto."

"Crowley again?" Andy questioned. Megan was almost insulted he had never heard those words before.

"Nope," Megan sat up straight, proud of herself. "LaVey."

"LaVey?" Andy questioned.

"Founder of Satanism," Megan explained the information she was making up. "Anton Szandor LaVey. Who better to summon a demon?"

"Wow," Andy seemed legitimately impressed. "You must really be taking Dr. Bringer's lessons to heart."

"Kind of," Megan giggled softly. "Ready to do this?"

"Yeah." Andy nodded.

Megan took his hands in hers and pretended to focus. Andy followed along. After a few deep calming breaths, Megan began to wonder why she was leading this whole thing.

"Klaatu," They began, "Barada Nikto!"

Nothing happened. The same voices came from outside muffled.

"I think we need to do it louder," Megan announced. "Maybe whatever is forming our demon didn't hear us."

"KLAATU!" They shouted. "BARADA! NIKTO!"

Again, nothing happened.

"One more time." Megan continued aggravated.

"KLAATU!!" This time the two were even louder. "BARADA!! NIKTO!!"

A light flashed outside. The shortly after a yell from a woman that sounded vaguely like "asshole" came from outside. Trash cans sounded like they were being knocked over and thrown around.

"What was that?" Andy rushed to the window to see a leg sticking out of a pile of knocked over aluminum garbage cans. "It wasn't like that before. I think there is someone out there."

"Of course, it wasn't like that before," Megan excitedly threw on her jacket to rush outside. "We did it together. It was stronger."

The two were out the door in no time, confronting whatever was in the trash cans outside. A horned and tattooed woman, who was very scantily clad in a black leather corset and leather skirt, laid still amongst the cans. Megan wanted to reach out and touch her but backed away in fear. She then motioned for Andy to touch her and make sure she was alright. Megan then hid behind Andy for protection.

The horned woman groaned when Andy's hand touched her bare leg. Slowly, she stirred and climbed out of the wreckage. She brushed herself off and stood up straight.

"Are you my master?" The horned woman spoke. Her sharp fangs glistened in the sun. "Are you the one who summoned me?"

Megan did everything she could to stifle a laugh at the overacting being done before her. Luckily, Andy was too transfixed on the sultry looking succubus before him.

"Yes," Andy acknowledged. "So is she."

"What is your bidding," The horned woman bowed slightly, "my master?"

"Uh…" Andy could not think of anything.

"Spin three times, and bark like a dog." Megan quickly shot out. She could not help herself. It would not be everyday she would have a demon to do her bidding. Even if the demon was just acting.

Without a hint of hesitation, the demon began to spin and bark.

"Holy shit," Andy exclaimed. "This one actually listens. Umm…let's go inside. We don't want anyone seeing her."

Andy led the way. The demon held her hands behind her back as she walked behind him. Megan took up the rear. The demon's right hand folded up into a middle finger behind her back. Megan did her best to stifle a giggle.

"So, what do we do with her?" Andy asked looking at the two women in the room. Megan walked around the demon gently touching her arms and shoulders examining her.

"I thought we had a plan." Megan put her chin on the demon's shoulder, giving a coy look to Andy.

"You're right." Andy remembered. The excitement had made him stop thinking with his brain. "Umm... I don't know where to begin."

"I have a very, very wicked idea." Megan seductively smiled as she moved closer to Andy.

"Ok." Andy was losing blood to his brain again.

"Why don't you sell her?" Megan suggested.

"We can't have that three-way first?" Andy quickly asked, slightly disappointed.

"Let me explain," Megan moved over to the demon. "You want back on the good side of that mage, right?"

Andy nodded.

"Now," Megan began to run a finger up the outer thigh of the demon and up to her hip, gently lifting the edge of the leather skirt. "You don't think she will get you back in her good graces? As part of the purchase price, you, me and her get time whenever we want. We don't need to keep her a secret from your parents as she has somewhere to go. Besides, Andy, I'm not a clean and nice girl. Getting fucked in a dirty place like that would be such a huge turn on."

Andy nodded. He reached towards his desk for his cell phone and made a call. He left the room and shut the door behind him.

"You ok?" Alegra whispered to Megan. The young woman did not waste the moment and tossed the leather book in her purse.

"I'm alright," Megan confirmed. "Aside from having to lick the inside of his mouth."

"I am so sorry, kid," Alegra cringed and gave Megan a sympathetic look. "At least Jon didn't surprise you by picking you up and throwing you into a bunch of trash cans."

"He owes both of us for this." Megan pulled a piece of garbage off a buckle on the back of Alegra's corset.

"He's coming," Alegra instructed Megan, "back to character."

Andy came back into the room.

"I just talked to the lady's subordinate," Andy put his phone in his pocket. "He says she'll be extremely interested. We'll take my car, but we need a way to make sure she isn't going to be an issue."

"Awesome," Megan got excited. Megan reached into a pocket of her jacket and pulled out a pair of handcuffs. "I brought these for our night, but I think they just found another use."

Andy swallowed hard as he watched Megan handcuff the demon's hands behind her back. The three walked down the stairs and to the garage to Andy's car. Megan helped the demon in the back of the car and got in the back with her. Andy got in the front and started the car. He pressed a button on the visor and the garage door opened. He backed out of the driveway. After getting the car on the road, the three were on their way.

Chapter 21

The car pulled up to an old burned out strip club. A few thugs were standing outside; presumably waiting for the trio as they parked and prepared to exit the car. Andy stepped out of the car first and opened the back door to let the demon out. Her high heeled boots made it a little hard to walk on the loose gravel, but Megan climbed out and helped the woman stay steady.

The guards approached the three and stopped them before they came too close. Andy held up his hands and the guards searched him. They approached the demon and searched her too, spending extra time checking her breasts and buttocks. The demon did not even flinch. Megan was next. When the guards moved to her chest, Andy tried to protest but they just shoved him to the ground gruffly. Megan bit her tongue as they felt her up and pinched a few things they probably should not have. She kept her cool as she remembered why she was doing this.

The guards got what they wanted and motioned for the three to head inside the club. The acrid smell of old burned wood, plastic, and cheap velvet filled Megan's nostrils, making her cough as they moved to the main room.

A pale woman in a long, tight, black, elegant dress stood looking at the burned wreckage of the club. A man, with his greasy looking hair, pulled back in a ponytail and an eyepatch was showing her around. The eye patch he wore tied the sliminess together. Megan also could not help but be disgusted by his obviously never washed polyester suit. She had figured that "dry clean only" must have been too expensive for him.

"Andy," The man turned to the group and gave a toothy, vile grin. For the first time since Megan took on this case, she truly feared for her life. It was not the guards with guns. It was not the building that was about to collapse, but it was something about the man in front of them. It was the way his eyes looked dead inside despite all the horrific things he had probably done. It was the way he tried to make everyone think they were comfortable. The fact of the matter was though, their lives did not matter at all to him. "Which one is the hottie for sale?"

"The demon." Andy spoke trying to give himself an air of authority. The crack in his voice broke his guise. "The one with the horns."

The gowned woman did not walk, but more glided over to the demon. The woman used her finger to gently lift the demon's chin and looked her over. She pulled a small pen knife out of her sleeve and put a nick in the skin of the horned woman. A small drop of blood dripped out before the wound quickly closed itself. The pale woman licked the blood up, and her eyes grew wide and she nodded.

"She's not an illusion." The woman spoke softly.

"Countess." The man with the ponytail motioned for the woman in the dress to step aside with him. The two discussed something in as private as they could manage in the room. The Countess returned and her features softened.

"Andrew." The woman in charge placed a hand on the side of Andy's cheek. "Young, magnificent Andrew. You have outdone yourself this time."

"You're in for a big payday, kid." The man with the ponytail clapped Andy on the shoulder, hard. "We don't know how you summoned this bitch, but we've been after for her for a few weeks now."

"What?" Andy was confused.

"Isn't that right," The man with the ponytail turned to the demon, "Mistress Valentine?"

Alegra had instantly recognized Grool as soon as they had walked in the strip club. The woman, however, was not someone she had ever met before. Alegra was able to guess that she was the blood mage in charge of the whole operation based on how Grool was essentially bowing to her.

"How you doing, Grool?" Alegra tried to stare into Max's soul with a wicked smirk on her lips. She had been holding it in the entire time, and it felt good to let out. "You look like you healed up well. Nasty scar though. How'd you get that?"

"That's what happens," Max pointed out a large scar on his neck. "When you some bitch makes a snack out of you. Lucky for me, my boss turned me into a vampire. Healed me right up. I'd offer you another taste, but I don't know how well vamp blood mixes with you."

"The last goon you sent me mixed just fine," Alegra licked her lips. "Still got him in my freezer if you want some."

"I'll pass." Grool walked away from Alegra. "However, I can't wait to drink whatever blood comes out of you."

"You might have to wait on that, Grool." A new male voice filled the room and was quickly followed by footsteps. Jon adjusted his glasses as he approached Grool.

"Well," Max spat angrily, "wondered if…"

"Shut up for a second," Jon pointed a finger at Grool before he walked up to the Countess and stuck his hand out and introduced himself. The woman just stared at him.

"Right, I don't think giving you a grip on me would be a good idea." Jon turned around and faced Grool once more but continued to address the woman. "You really hired this guy? You should have a better taste in employees. I mean, a vampire that can't even regenerate a body part? That's just sad."

Jon then patted Grool on the shoulder.

"I'm talking about you, buddy." Jon pointed at Grool. "You suck at being a vampire. Couldn't even kick my ass. How much blood have you even drank? Drop? Maybe two? How sick did it make you? Let me ask you, did she even tell you what she really is? You still think both of you are vampires?"

"I've…" Grool began.

"Maybe a little more blood might help." Jon held out his wrist. "You're possibly ravenous. Might not be able to help yourself. Go ahead. Let's see those fangs. Come on. Bring them out. What? You don't have any?"

"What is Jon doing?" Megan whispered to no one in particular.

"Running his mouth," Alegra responded flatly. Megan could only get a glimpse of Alegra's arms gently jostling behind herself. "It's what he does best."

214

"And you must be Andy." Jon took the young man's hand, where it hung limply at Andy's side, and shook it. "You should be proud of yourself. Interesting creatures you can summon. However, you need to stop thinking with your dick. You let Megan lead every single one of you into this trap. You did this all for a pair of tits. Congrats."

"I don't see a trap here, Mr. Bringer," the Countess spoke. "You seem to be heavily outnumbered here."

"Doctor," Jon corrected her. "My god, and you. Out of everyone here, you have got to be the most cliché, and pathetic excuse for a villainous mage I have ever met. This is coming from a very shitty necromancer. I can't even raise a zombie. I doubt you can even control blood enough to kill me where I stand. Hell, when I told the Library about you. You know what they said?"

"I..." The Countess began.

"I'll tell you," Jon held up a finger in her face. "You weren't even worth their time. Funny enough, I have a friend that works very closely with the FBI. You aren't even worth investigating on their end too. All these guards, all these guns, and they're ready to die for a nobody. You know, I thought you might have at least looked interesting. You are so much of a generic movie villain. I bet you call yourself 'Countess Elizabeth.'"

"I am a sanguaniress," The woman became visibly upset, "and I do not appreciate your mocking tone."

"Mage?" Grool's confusion about what Jon was talking about boiled to the front of his mind.

"Then stop being such a try-hard." Jon stood in front of her. "Go ahead. Kill me. I've drank a small bit of your blood from your goon. Make me pop. You can do it. Come on. Pop! You'll make my wife extremely happy and save her on a divorce lawyer. Come on, make something pop. I believe in you!"

A scowl came across Countess "Elizabeth's" face. Grool began to turn red and his eye began to bug out. Soon, his face changed shade to purple and blood began to pour out his nose. After a few more seconds, his chest exploded, sending shards of bone and blood all over the room. Jon noticed a small, extra hot, drop had landed on his lip. Wanting to test something, Jon gave it a quick lick. Ash.

"Perfect," Jon nodded to himself." You just proved another theory of mine. You have been telling Grool that your blood made him a vampire. After having him drink, you were able to control his body. You even healed him. Let me ask. Did you ever tell him you weren't a vampire, or did you just let him die thinking you were much more powerful than you really were? I think his confused look right before he died answers that question quite well. You really are pathetic."

"Kill him!" The Countess shouted.

All the guards in the room pulled their triggers at the same time. Jon did not even attempt to move as none of the guns went off.

"You don't even listen," Jon scoffed at the woman, "or pay attention. Do you know what a poltergeist is? It's a spirit that is a bit mischievous. Moves things in your house. Surprisingly, very docile, and common as far as spirits go. Do you know what they especially enjoy? Shiny objects. You'd be amazed at what they would do for the baubles in those guns while I run my mouth and distract everyone."

All the guards checked their submachine guns. The magazines were not in the weapons just as Jon had said. They laid on the ground, empty. The blood mage began to back up, clearly intimidated.

"You guys may want to reload." Jon turned to all the guards. "I think our demon friend is free."

As if on cue, Alegra handed the handcuffs that were keeping her restrained to Andy.

"Next time," Alegra smiled a jagged, violent grin at the young man. "Don't try to restrain a dominatrix with toy bedroom cuffs. Quick releases make these things useless."

This bit of time was all the guards needed to reload and open fire. Jon quickly tackled Megan, making sure she was on the ground, and under the flying lead. Alegra leaped at one of the guards and slammed him to the floor. With her hands clasped around the guard's neck, cutting off his oxygen, she lowered her head to take a bite.

Another guard came running and punted the woman in the ribs. Before he could pull the trigger on his gun a ghastly, ethereal face gave a shrill cry sending pain into his ears before he could. The momentary startle gave Alegra a chance to kick the guard's leg out from under him. Alegra ripped at the guard's fingers on his weapon trying to get it away from him. After that failed, the use of her teeth on his wrist's tendons did the trick. She then turned and shot at a guard aiming at Jon; missing but causing the guard to duck and not take his shot.

Megan belly crawled along the ground to find cover. Bullets whizzed overhead. She felt her heart rate pound higher than it had ever been in her life. After crawling behind the bar, she waited, crouched down as low as she could. A few stray shots punctured her cover and smashed into the glasses still on the shelf. Everything felt so similar to the fight in Misshapen, but something about it was different this time. She had a dog in this fight too. Megan looked around and grabbed glasses and bottles of booze.

"Eat it, asshole!" Megan popped out from behind the bar and threw a glass at a guard pointing his weapon at Alegra.

Andy crawled after Megan and reached to her in fear. Soot and dirt-covered both of them. Megan looked down at the man clutching her leg. Tears ran down his face; he was frightened. She wanted to laugh but realized not everyone dealt with life or death situations as well as she was faking it right now. Hell, had it been a few weeks ago, she might have been right there with him. Now, she felt she could do something, or as the adrenaline running through her body was telling her, she could do anything.

Megan motioned for him to stay down and continued her volley of projectiles. Bullets came her way, missing and shattering the liquor bottles behind her. When they stopped Megan returned fire with whatever had not been destroyed.

Jon dusted himself off a bit and noticed the Countess used Grool's blood to create a spear and fling it at Alegra. The demon saw it coming and with a lithe backward jump, dodged the attack. The projectile shattered harmlessly against the floor. The woman aimed a second attack, but this time the body of another mage slammed into her, throwing her to the floor.

One thing that Jon had always noticed in his violent encounters with other mages, was that they always relied too heavily on their powers. This was a weakness Jon wanted to exploit as much as he could. He had taken mixed martial arts classes and had become proficient in both jujitsu and wrestling.

With little effort, Jon was on top of the Countess and began to rain punches down on her. A few blows landed home on her shoulders and her forearms as she blocked them. She twisted her body out of the way the best she could. Nothing landed the knockout Jon was aiming for. The blood mage grabbed his arm as it came down for another punch and a searing pain shot through it. The burning sensation sent

Jon to the ground clutching the affected appendage, as he began to feel it spread up his arm.

While Jon fought the Countess and Alegra took on the armed guards, a lone guard broke away from the battle and made his way behind the counter of the bar. Megan threw a bottle his way, knocking the gun out of his hand and to the ground. The guard shoved Andy out of the way and came straight for Megan. She recognized him immediately as the guard that had groped her and Alegra earlier.

"What's the matter, little girl?" The guard snarled as he grabbed Megan by the collar and lifted her up to face him. Megan tried to wrestle free but, with a forceful shove the guard threw her. In an attempt to regain her balance, she tripped over Andy and hit the ground. "Didn't enjoy being felt up by a real man?"

Megan did not even respond. As he crept closer, Megan threw a kick at the man's testicles. The guard just swatted the attack away. He responded with a backhand across Megan's face, knocking her back to the floor.

"I'll teach you some fucking respect." The guard reached down to grab Megan but was stopped in his tracks. A pair of tattooed arms wrapped around the man's neck. Alegra used the leverage of controlling the guard's head to wrestle him to the ground on his stomach. The man coughed and sputtered as Alegra mounted him. However, something in her froze and caused her to loosen her grip. The man flipped around and struck a punch to her jaw, but it barely phased her. Bullet holes marred Alegra's back; some were still bleeding, and some had already stopped. Alegra didn't want to let herself go again. She didn't want her to see her true nature again this close, and possibly run her off for good.

"Alegra," Megan's voice called over the sound of the battle. Alegra turned back to see Megan climbing back to her feet. She wiped a small trickle of blood off her lip. "Bite his fucking dick off."

That was all the demon needed to hear. She bared her teeth and drove them into the man's throat. He made a strange noise as he screamed until his larynx was crush in the woman's jaws.

The man did not squirm or writhe as much as the last one Megan saw Alegra kill. Megan made sure to not look away this time. She had told herself before walking back into the bar that this was her reality now. This was what she had to face. Every time had to be easier than the last.

"She just ate that guy's throat," Andy cried out in fear. Terror froze the next words from coming out.

"She's a demon." Megan looked down at Andy, who now how a large wet spot on his crotch. "What did you expect?"

The Countess had bolted from the main room to the back before Jon made it back to his feet. His left arm, where the mage had touched him, was numb. Holes were left in his flesh. A few bled slightly, but the majority appeared cauterized shut. The magic touch had stopped at his shoulder. He could only hope that it would become useful again soon. Right now, though, he didn't have the luxury of worrying about it. The back hallway where she had run was a straight shot to the back door. This was exactly where the mage was headed, and Jon was right behind her.

"Elizabeth" made it to the door and tried frantically fiddled with the lock to open it. The door opened easier than she was expecting. Where she was expecting freedom, however, a tall, sharply dressed man who stood in her way. His dreadlocks were tied neatly behind his head and that made it easy for Jon to recognize him in the moonlight; it was Malcolm, the vampire he had met earlier.

"Excuse me, ma'am." Malcolm pushed past the two and made his way to the main room.

The Countess did not let this opportunity pass her by and rushed into the night behind the door. The woman turned to kick at Jon who was rushing her. Fighting in heels left her off balance and not fast enough for the kick to be a threat. Jon caught her foot and picked her up, slamming her into the ground, hard. The woman coughed and sputtered. Jon now sat on her chest. The woman did her best to block the punches coming at her but, thanks to her lack of conditioning, was failing. So, she instead grabbed him by the side of his shirt and threw it up over his head, tangling Jon up. She then reached out and grabbed Jon's bare chest. An intense burning sensation filled his chest as she began to dig her fingers into Jon's skin.

Jon swatted her hand away, tearing away a slight bit of his skin in the process. With her hands parried away, Jon dropped an elbow across the woman's temple, making a cut that began to bleed, and knocked her out. As he climbed off the woman and dusted himself off, he took a deep breath and sighed heavily. He considered landing a few more blows to make sure she would be out for a while but thought better of it. He wanted to stop her, not kill her or leave her brain damaged. Instead, he pulled his belt off and wrapped the woman's arms behind her back.

Jon headed back to the club. The sound of gunfire began to die off slowly as he approached the main room.

When he entered, Malcolm was surveying the fallen. Alegra was crouched over one, tearing away at the still barely living flesh. When the body she was devouring would stop moving, she moved on to the next dying man. Jon figured it was best not to interrupt her.

"Which one is Grool?" Malcolm approached Jon. "I've checked for teeth. I've checked for just piles of ash. There is none of it."

"Grool is over there." Jon pointed to what was left of the man who did not live long enough to see the battle begin. "Our blood mage friend killed him before you even showed up. Thing is, he wasn't a vampire. Countess in the back just led him to believe that so that she could manipulate him further after she saved him from death. Frankly, the poor bastard got out lucky."

"This is the problem with you mages," The vampire scoffed at the necromancer. "You use others like they are nothing but playthings."

"I guess we're not too different," Jon sarcastically retorted as he checked the damage on his body. "I remember a certain vampire telling me all about how all blood sharing was just a way to control mortals."

"Jon?" Megan's voice called out from behind the bar.

"Come on out," Jon called back. "Might want to cover your eyes. Alegra is already doing her thing."

"I know," Megan slowly climbed out from behind the bar. "I already saw her. Predator to prey. I get it."

Megan slowly crept up to Alegra, who was lost in the ecstasy of fresh meat. Megan still wanted to vomit from what she was witnessing, but this time was different. She always heard that seeing a dead body got easier every time you see one. True enough, this time was easier than the last. She wondered how she would feel about the next one. Would she ever get so used to it that she would be able to kill if she had to? She admitted to herself that was not a thought she liked.

"You're ok seeing this?" Jon asked. He gently touched her shoulder to warn of his presence as Megan watched on, entranced.

"It's actually," Megan leaned in closer, "intriguing. Like watching a snake hunt. Kind of a funny feeling not being on the top of the food chain."

"If it helps," Jon shrugged. "You never were. It's more like a big circle. At some point in our lives, something eats everyone. Alegra just does it while they're still pretty much whole."

"Uh, guys," Andy's voice called out as he stood up from behind the bar. "A little help. Megan?"

Jon motioned over to Andy with his head. Megan just looked over and shrugged. She went back to watching Alegra eat.

"Hey," Malcolm's voice interrupted all of them. "I think we have a problem."

Alegra was the second one to notice, after Malcolm. The blood from the body she was eating began to drain. All the pools and spots on the walls began to move and slide. Everything was melting into one central point in the club. Instinctively, Alegra stood between the now pooling blood and the mortals of the group. Two gargantuan hands made entirely of blood began to emerge from the pool. The huge, viscous hands used the floor to pull the rest of their body up. Next a head, elongated and toothy, began to come up. Even though it had no eyes, it was easy to see hatred, and violence were the only things on its mind.

Jon looked over his shoulder. The Countess waved a hand in the air. He figured the blood that came from her head was enough for her to manipulate the belt and free herself. As she motioned, the creature made of blood began to stir and move along with motions of her hand.

"Giant blood golem." Malcolm looked at the growing monstrosity.

"Looks to me like a snack." Alegra grinned a toothy, animalistic grin.

"You're going to get fat eating that." Malcolm looked at the demon.

"I can run it off." Alegra launched herself at the monster and after latching on, sunk her teeth in deeply. The creature roared and attempted to throw her off. Malcolm followed suit and lunged at the living blood pool.

"Wait," Jon turned to the Countess, who was now using a pillar in the doorway to hold herself up. She was concussed, and her non-focused eyes told Jon she was barely even there. She would not able to have total control of the spell and Jon knew it. "There is no need for more violence. Listen to me."

The Countess continued to grow the monster.

"What do you plan to accomplish at this point?" Jon rushed to the woman's side as she began to collapse. Jon held her weight and helped her sit on the floor. "You're summoning something that big after a concussion. Are you trying to kill yourself?"

"And take you all with me," The woman coughed.

"What's the point?" Jon sat down with the woman. "You kill us, and you become helpless in the process of calling that thing. After they kill that thing, you have an angry vampire and demon ready to tear you limb from limb while you're still alive. Very shitty proposition if you ask me. The authorities and the Library are already on to you even if you did escape. I've made sure of that in case this all failed. However, if you give yourself up and put the creature back, you'll get to live. You'll do some time, maybe even none depending on what crime they tag you for. Then you get to go back to living your life."

"There is no life for me after this." The blood mage stopped moving her hand.

"That's not true," Jon debated her train of thought. "Look, blood mages are not necessarily an enemy. The

224

Library doesn't have a kill on sight order. It's the actions that many take that have led them to have problems with the authorities. Hell, I'm a necromancer. We used to be grave robbers, and all that fun stuff. Torturing people to find that spot between life and death. What you are is not who you are. Give yourself up. I'll help you."

"Who are you?" the blood mage laughed weakly, "My shrink?"

"I am a doctor of parapsychology," Jon surmised, "and psychology is in that big word."

The woman shrugged and threw her hands up. Jon had a good point and she knew it. The creature disappeared instantly into a pool of blood, dropping Alegra and Malcolm to the ground.

"Andy!" Jon called out. "That's his name, right Megan?"

Megan nodded.

"Andy," Jon motioned to the young man who was slowly climbing to his feet. "Come here. I need you to help me."

Andy slowly made his way across the room to Jon. Each step was deliberate and cautious to make sure nothing was going happen to him. Alegra fake lunged at him when he got close. Andy yelped in fear and fell to the ground. He looked to Megan for reassurance but did not find the friendly, seductive face from earlier. She just stared at him on the ground, cold and disgusted. She reached back to kick him and thought better of it when the young man tried to protect himself.

"That's enough, guys," Jon scolded the two of them. "Andy, they won't hurt you. Please, come here."

Andy got back to his feet and made his way to Jon.

"What do you need?" Andy asked quietly.

"You had a very big part in this whole mess," Jon looked at the young man. "You were playing with powers you didn't understand. I need you to help clean up this mess. Can you do that for me?"

Andy looked around at all the carnage. He knew that this was kicked off by him selling something he didn't even understand, nor wanted. People were hurt and lives were lost. Millions of dollars in damages had occurred and he was in the middle of it all.

"Am I going to jail?" Andy squeaked, looking around.

"I don't know," Jon admitted to the young man, who now looked to be nothing more than a scared boy. "I'm not the police. What I do know, is the people that investigate this sort of thing are on their way. What I need you to do is make sure she doesn't leave." He pointed towards the Countess.

"We all need to leave. We can't be here when they arrive. Can you take care of her for us? If you do this for us, I'll talk to them and do what I can to get them to go easy on you. I know you didn't know what you were doing. You don't need to be punished. You need guidance."

"You could teach me," Andy begged, "Then we all could leave together."

"No," Jon shook his head. "I'm not the person to train you. If it were up to me, I'd do whatever I could to make sure you couldn't use magic again. You have no respect for living things. You have no respect for the lives you created. You're lucky I don't leave you alone with the demon. Do you understand?"

Andy nodded.

"Good," Jon stood up. "You alright, Alegra?"

The demon nodded. Her bullet holes were almost already gone. Jon knew he was going to have to help pull the actual bullets out later, but for right now, making sure she was alright was an important priority.

"Let's get out of here," Alegra spoke. Her eyes had returned to normal, but her voice still had a violent growl to it.

"Wait," Megan stopped Jon as the three began to leave. She walked up to Andy. "Andy, I need your car keys quick. I snuck the book out with me when we left. I need to get it from the car. It might have some information that will help us with Miko."

"Miko?" Andy questioned.

"The cat girl you summoned," Megan explained to him. "She has a name. She has a home now, but she still needs help. We don't know exactly what she is. Jon and I are fairly certain she is not a familiar, but we need that book to know for sure."

Andy nodded. He reached in his pocket and pulled out his car keys and handed them to Megan. Megan ran out and within a minute, ran back in. In her arms, she carried the leather-bound book she and Andy read from together.

"I wish I could say I was sorry about using you," Megan started, "but I'm not. Don't ever contact me again."

Andy nodded in agreement.

Book in hand, she led her two friends out of the building.

Malcolm looked around.

"Well," Malcolm shrugged as he left. "This was a waste of my time."

Andy and the woman were alone. As he looked once more at the wreckage, and he felt tears well up.

"You're lucky," The blood mage spoke up and broke the silence. "Those people sounded like they are seriously looking out for you. They sound tough, but if he wanted you dead, he would have let that woman feast. I wish I had someone who would have helped me in the beginning. Maybe I wouldn't have ended up this way. Tell you what, Andy..."

"I'm not letting you go." Andy shook his head.

"I'm not asking you too," The Countess groaned as she righted herself. "Dr. Bringer there didn't sound too sure about us having any trouble with the authorities. Maybe we should take his advice and seek that guidance. I mean, he's right. If a necromancer can be as thoughtful as he is, maybe there is hope for us."

"Yeah," Andy nodded. "Maybe you're right."

Chapter 22

Jon sat at the bar at Misshapen, slowly nursing the drink in his hand. His body still ached from the fight a few days ago. He had already dropped a glass tonight trying to get control back in his left arm. He assumed it would be back in time. That did not mean he could not help the process along by trying to use it.

Megan had gone to her dorm and had not shown up for class the one-day Jon had it taught since then. He did not mind. He understood.

"Moving slow, old man." Alegra put another beer in front of Jon even though he had not finished the one he had.

"You think I'm going to need another one after this?" Jon chuckled.

"Jon," Alegra leaned on the counter. "I've known you since we were seventeen. You are a man of your vices. Now, if only I could just get you to stop smoking. I don't think an electronic voice box would look good on you."

Jon smiled slightly as he waved off her comment.

"Neither would a liver transplant scar," Jon downed the beer he had, "but here we are."

"Got to pay for this place somehow." Alegra reconciled with herself.

The door to the bar opened. A young man in a black band shirt walked in carrying a heavy black suitcase. He did not even stop for the bouncer deep into her reading.

"Whit!" Alegra yelled. "Are you even carding people anymore? He looks way too young to be here."

Whit's just gave Alegra a thumbs up from her seat, acknowledging that she heard the question. She never even looked up from her book.

"Uh," the young man started. "Where can I set this up?"

"Who the hell are you?" Alegra squinted her eyes, confused. "What do you think you're doing?"

"I'm the sound guy," The man spoke as he noticed the stage and set his suitcase on it. He opened it and began pulling equipment out, not waiting for Alegra to answer him.

"Ok, Mr. Sound Guy," Alegra was getting upset. "That still doesn't answer my second question."

"I'm setting up the mixing, so everything sounds alright." He walked onto the stage and moved to the amplifiers that flanked the sides of the stage. They were not big, but he figured they would do. "Do these even work?"

"No idea," Jon answered him. "Never been used."

"Do you know something about this?" Alegra turned to Jon. Jon just shook his head and went back to his beer.

Soon, a few more people walked in. Two with guitar cases and one with a few smaller cases, all paraded in. Alegra could only guess that it was a drum kit.

"Alright," Alegra stormed around from behind the bar and approached the people at the stage. "Someone needs to answer me what the hell is going on here. If no one does, I'm calling the cops."

"Our singer said they talked to the owner of this place," One of the guys with a guitar case explained. "Booked us to play here."

"So, you do know something about this." Alegra turned to Jon.

"Of course, Jon does." Caine chimed in coming back to his seat from the restroom. He swirled the little bit left in his glass before finishing the last swallow.

"She can get a little too fired up, huh?" Caine joked with Jon.

"If only you knew." Jon took a drink from his beer.

"She going to be pissed about whatever you set up here?" Caine pointed his thumb over his right shoulder towards the stage.

"She'll add it to the list." Jon got up and poured a beer for Caine and slid it to the tall man.

"So," Caine started after taking a drink. "You said you wanted to talk to me."

"What did you guys find at the club?" Jon asked.

"The blood mage was slumped in the corner," Caine recollected. "She was talking to a young man. Both were smiling and sharing stories. FBI took both. They're trying to figure out what to do with them. I don't think anything is going to happen to the kid. Miko is a familiar and all that jazz."

"You're wrong," Jon smiled a victorious smile. "Steve was wrong. I got a hold of the book Andy used to summon her. A familiar has no actual will of its own, and it only wants to serve its master. She might be naïve, but she does have her own thoughts and emotions. So, I read the book. She's just a regular, old, summoned creature. That guy made life. Steve almost shit when I told him. Had nothing happened, who knows what he could have summoned and then couldn't control. He tried summoning a damn succubus…"

"That's' what we need," Caine laughed, "another demon."

"My thoughts exactly," Jon smiled, looking at Alegra who was trying to control what was going on with her stage. "One is enough damn trouble."

"So, the kid actually did break laws and accords," Caine rubbed his chin. "I should let the feds know. Let them deal with him. I don't want to have to kill a guy that young."

"Leave him alone," Jon requested from behind his beer. "Do you want to kick off a war between you fine folks and The Library? They are going to try and get their hands on him as soon as they can find him. For someone that can make creatures like her? I can see a large body count."

"That sounds like a massive pain in the ass," Caine admitted.

"You know," Jon chuckled, watching Alegra getting worked up. She eventually threw her hands up as the sound guy began a mic check and everyone started tuning up their instruments. "Contrary to how she's acting, you can kind of see her enjoying this."

"Fuck it!" Alegra exclaimed as she returned to her position behind the bar.

"Just calm down and enjoy the show," Jon finished off his drink. "You always wanted that stage used, and now it's going to happen."

"I don't even know who these people are!" Alegra protested hard. "I didn't audition them. I don't even know what they play."

"Music," Jon filled her in, "they play music."

"Oh, so that's why they gave you the doctorate." Alegra shook her head.

"She's pissed." Caine pointed out the obvious. "Did you ever figure out the ashy blood? Even to me, that was a bit of a new one."

"I have a good theory." Jon pulled back the bandage on his arm. "She was expelling so much energy trying to keep that body alive that she was burning up the blood. All just to confirm what her goons probably told her about our rescue mission."

"No vampires," Caine confirmed.

"Malcom showed up," Jon recounted. "He helped Alegra with the guards. He was also kind of upset that Grool was dead by the time he got there."

At this time, the door opened one more time and Megan walked in. Her outfit was different than what the group was used to. Chains and tight vinyl adorned her. Her makeup was heavy. Her eyes looked sunken. Her purple hair, which she tended to keep pulled back, was let free to flow around her shoulders. And no one was sure, but it looked like she had at least one new piercing.

"This shit set up yet?" Megan called out to the band.

"Wanna get your ass up here and help?" The drummer yelled back.

"Rather get up there and fucking rock." Megan turned back to the bar. It was obvious that the gears in Alegra's head were turning. Jon got up and walked around the dumbfounded demon and poured a shot of top-shelf whiskey. Megan took it from him downed the shot and returned to the stage. The band was ready to go.

The drummer slammed his sticks together to the count of four and the instruments roared to life. Megan took her time. She listened to the music. It was fast, aggressive and ready for her. She could feel it. She could feel it deep in every fiber of her being. Her vocals came out soft, symphonic, but matched everything, giving a jagged yet beautiful juxtaposition. When the chorus came, her vocals turned to a roar. Scratchy, violent, and full of energy.

Jon could not help but smile watching Alegra enjoy the music. She was entranced. Slowly, she lost herself and where she was. She stopped running the bar and became a listener. Megan and her band continued. More force, more drive, more desire. Their audience was small, but it was theirs and it was their opportunity to put on their show.

When the music stopped Jon and Caine clapped from their seats. Alegra stood there. In all the years she had run the bar, she had but one desire. She wanted people to use that stage to express themselves. She did not care how. She wanted the office worker who hated their 9 to 5 to become a rock star. She wanted the socially unattractive to dance and become desired. She wanted to let the introvert belt out their poetry. Her golden eyes began to well up. The band took a second. Alegra climbed on stage and stared down at the smaller lead singer.

"Sorry," Megan apologized. "Should have asked first. Jon said it was cool."

Alegra said nothing. She could not. The woman only took Megan in her arms and wrapped her in a warm embrace. Megan returned it. Then let go.

"Being all emotional at one song?" Megan smiled at her friend. "You?"

"Shut up, kid." Alegra got off the stage and went back to the bar. She tried to hide it, but the demon was glowing. There was only one other time in her life she was happier than this, but this came in as a close second.

"Where's Miko?" Megan looked around and hopped off the stage.

"She hasn't been downstairs in a while," Alegra explained. "Someone had said somethings that made her uncomfortable and she's been hiding upstairs ever since."

"I didn't say anything." Caine defended himself as Megan glared at him.

"Can I go try and talk to her?" Megan asked. "This is for her too."

Alegra grabbed her keys and handed them to Megan.

"Good luck." Alegra motioned for her to make the way through without going outside.

"I'll be back guys," Megan turned towards her band after heading towards the stairway's door. "Everything sounded off. Mike, can you give us another soundcheck?"

"Our little Miss Mousey has become a little bossy, wouldn't you say?" Caine smiled to himself. "Sounds like she's been taking lessons from someone."

Megan found the apartment dark. She wished she had paid attention to where the lights were but trusted Miko to come to her.

"Miko?" Megan called out.

"What?" The cat woman's voice came from the bedroom. Megan pulled out her phone and turned on the flashlight feature and found the light switch. She then walked into the bedroom where Miko lay on the bed. She looked like she had not changed or showered in days. On top of that, she was very pale.

"You ok?" Megan sat down on the bed next to Miko. She gently touched the cat woman on the back. The woman arched her back into the touch.

"No." Miko shook her head.

"Why not?" Megan put her hands in her lap. "My band is downstairs playing and we want you to come hear us."

"Why?" The cat woman shrugged the idea off.

"Because we're all down there enjoying ourselves and want you to come and have fun with us." Megan felt slightly silly explaining this to her.

"People don't want me around." Miko turned away from Megan.

"What on Earth gives you that idea?" Megan felt offended but did not let it show. "I mean, I'm up here telling you I want you around."

"I'm just a familiar," Miko explained. "I'm meant to be used, sold, abused and slaughtered when I'm not good enough anymore. I'm disposable. Even the person who created me didn't want me."

Megan did not know what to say. She had the words inside her, but she did not know how to let them out properly. It took her a minute, but she found them.

"Can I tell you a secret?" Megan looked over at Miko, as she sat down on the bed with her. Miko nodded. "You can't tell anyone this."

"Ok." Miko sat up listening intently, but still not making eye contact.

"The people who created me didn't want me either," Megan explained. "When I was born, whoever gave birth to me gave me up for adoption. I never knew them. I never knew why they didn't want me. Why they just threw me away. It hurt. It hurt a lot when I found this out. Was I not good enough? Was it because I was a girl instead of boy? So many thoughts. So many unanswered questions. So, I know where you are coming from. You know what though?"

"Hmm...?" Miko was listening harder now.

"I found people who did want me. I was adopted by two loving people in Chicago named Barbra and Paul. They raised me as if they gave birth to me. They raised me right along with their son. There was no difference between us. No one got more presents at Christmas. No one got scolded harder. We were both their children. They loved both of us equally. What I'm getting at is sometimes, the people that you're supposed to think of as your family, aren't. This seems like one of those cases. Andy didn't want you. Grool and him abused you. But right now, you have Jon, Alegra, and me, and we want you around. I know it hurts to not be wanted. I stopped looking at the people who didn't want me, and sure enough, I was able to see the ones that did a lot better."

Miko sat up and stretched. Megan looked at the cat warmly. She wrapped her arms around her and then let go. Megan stood up.

"I'm headed back down," Megan told her. "If you want to come down. Come down. We're going to rock this place so hard it might get busy tonight. I know Alegra will need help."

"Megan," Miko softly asked. "What will I do when Jon and Alegra don't want me anymore?"

"First," Megan smiled at the woman. She wiped a small tear that appeared on Miko's face away. "If they ever make that decision, I'm kicking both their asses. Then, you're coming to live with me. Got it?"

Miko nodded. Megan left the apartment and returned downstairs.

When Megan returned, she found the sound test had been over for a bit now. Alegra had propped the door open. Whit had a scowl on her face as she tried to fight the breeze from flipping the pages in her book.

Megan got back on stage and got ready for her next song. Before she could start, everyone's attention turned to the doorway of the back room. Miko stood there. She had not changed from the t-shirt and shorts she had been wearing. No one seemed to mind. She quickly grabbed up all of Jon and Caine's empty glasses and got back to work like normal.

The band began again, and everyone continued to enjoy the restful and quiet night.

<u>Epilogue</u>

Andy had not been back to Dr. Bringer's class. He couldn't bring himself too. After what he had done, and after what he had seen, he even considered dropping out of school altogether to avoid ever having to face him, or Megan.

Right now, the only place he spent his free time was at the library. He was able to get to class quickly, and back to the library to hide. He could bring his laptop, watch a movie. In truth, Andy had to admit to himself that he felt at ease here.

He had even begun to do his research. Looking into other creatures that he could summon. He would flip through the pages. Make notes and then stop. He didn't have the book anymore. What was the point for him to keep looking and hoping?

He would also look into the biographies of the various other magic users after reading the books on the people Megan had mentioned during their "summoning." Andy was nose deep in a book by Crowley now. Seated at a table alone, he flipped through the pages as he absorbed the knowledge within.

"Find a good read?" A deep male voice interrupted Andy's train of thought. "Crowley does have some good points, but sadly the majority of it is just fiction."

Andy looked up to see an older gentleman now seated at the table with him. He had not seen anyone enter the room in his peripheral vision. Nor had he heard the man slide the chair out and sit down.

"You're Andrew Spetz, correct?" The man smiled warmly and leaned back in the wooden chair. "My name is Steven LaGrange."

"Can I help you?" Andy stammered as he tried to hide a little deeper in his book.

"I'm here to help you, Andrew," Steve crossed his legs and folded his hands in his lap. "I heard about you from a mutual friend. Dr. Jonathan Bringer."

"I wouldn't call Dr. Bringer a friend." Andy slowly closed the book and set it down.

"Not many people would." Steve uncrossed his legs and leaned closer now that he knew he had the young man's attention. "He said you summoned an actual creature," "A cat woman. I met her too. I'm overly impressed with your work."

"I didn't do it." Andy's eyes began to bolt towards the door.

"No need to lie to me, Andrew," Steve reached in his pocket. "I'm not with the police. I'm not here with the FBI. I'm not here to hurt you. I'm here for just the opposite reason. I represent a group of mages. The largest group in the world. We call ourselves The Library. It's our goal to help wayward mages in their journey for knowledge. We helped Dr. Bringer when he first discovered his power. We would like to offer you the same opportunity"

"Jon said…" Andy began.

"Jon told me to come to talk to you," Steve interrupted Andy. "He wants me to help you as we helped him. You'll still live your normal life, but on top of that you will take a class here and there at The Library to help you hone your skills."

"I read a book about a school like that once." Andy began to feel more and more at ease.

"I'm sure you have," Steve smiled. "I'm your owl, Andy. Why don't you come with me and I'll show you the school?"

Andy did not know what to say. He checked his watch.

"I have class soon," Andy protested, "and I would need to run some sort of trip like this through my parents first. I would need to know how we're going…"

Andy stopped talking as Steve simply snapped his fingers and a large swirling portal appeared behind him.

"You'll be home in time for dinner," Steve stood up and began to walk towards the portal. "Come on, Andrew. This portal won't be open forever."

Andy stopped. He every fiber of his being was hesitant to follow the man into the vortex, but something in him could not stop. He grabbed his bag and steeled himself as best he could. This was a once in a lifetime opportunity, and it beat having to ever face Jon or Megan again.

Andy pushed in his chair and walked to the man standing by the purple portal. The man put his hand on Andy's shoulder to help reassure him that it would all be alright. The two then walked through together.

Jon sat down at his desk in his office. Megan opened the door with two foam cups of coffee from the campus cafe. She set Jon's on the desk. She popped off the top and pulled out her flask. She poured a bit into Jon's coffee, closed the lid, and put it back in her jacket. Jon just laughed at how well he had his employee trained.

"So, nothing is going to happen to Andy?" Megan asked, sipping her drink.

"No," Jon confirmed. "Long story short, I have a feeling The Library is going to try and recruit him. That's what's protecting him."

"Who knows?" Megan questioned. "Maybe he'll come back a new man."

"That tends to be what they do." Jon stared down at his cup. Megan felt an awkward silence between the two of them. She was not exactly sure what caused it, but she figured the talk about Andy's future wasn't helping the situation. She quickly decided to change the subject.

"So," Megan looked over at Jon, "am I an official part of the team?'

"Huh?" Jon was interrupted from his train of though. He did the best he could to act like nothing was on his mind and nodded. "Yeah. You seemed to get what we're doing with it. Caine told me how you told him to 'fuck off'."

"Sweet," Megan felt a swell of pride in herself. "What's next?"

"Well," Jon set down his drink and looked at the young woman. "I believe there is a voice in my head that you have completely forgotten about. A woman looking for her husband."

"Good," Megan nodded. "I could use a break from a bit of heavy action for a while."

"Me too, Megan," Jon nodded, "me too."

About the Author

Joshua Koehn began writing when his mother suggested he put pen to paper in an attempt to help with his depression. Lost in a town that he felt didn't understand him he found that this suggestion let him create his own worlds that he understood.

The first full length novel he wrote was a horrible collection of stories he jammed together called "A.O.D." Over the years, the stories came together from a mess into a cohesive tale. As such, Misshapen Angels was born.

Now, living in Chicago. Joshua found his tribe and found his home. Drinking terrible beer, petting his terrible dog, and living with his terrible girlfriend.

If there was one thing, he could tell his former self, and as a word to anyone still lost trying to find their way.

"Hang on, it gets better."

www.ingramcontent.com/pod-product-compliance
Lightning Source LLC
Chambersburg PA
CBHW020728210626
46807CB00016B/446